洞月亮
CAVE MOON PRESS
YAKIMA 中 WASHINGTON

2017

Byrd and the Bees

Byrd and the Bees

By

Christine McInerney Fry

If you think writing a Fairy Tale is hard…try living one.

洞月亮
CAVE MOON PRESS
YAKIMA 中 WASHINGTON

Byrd and the Bees

Cave Moon Press, P.O. Box 1773, Yakima, WA 98907
www.cavemoonpress.com

ISBN: 9780692825921
LCCN: 2016963455

To my Seester, Theresa

You made the world a better place.

Chapter 1

Sometimes Prince Charming is a prince. Sometimes he's actually a frog. And once in a while, good 'ole Prince Charming turns out to be a real bastard.

Cameron was a real bastard.

We worked together for about a year at Boltz Hardware and Garden in Martinsburg, West Virginia. I was in lumber. He was in lighting and fixtures. We often exchanged a flirtatious glance or a playful smirk across the aisles, and for a good portion of that time nothing progressed between us because he was dating Karen, one of our coworkers. As luck would have it, she transferred to a management position at a Home Fix-it near Reno, Nevada. I guess long-distance relationships weren't Cameron's thing because, within five minutes of her departure, he found me. He hopped onto the forklift I was operating, and said, "We should start seeing each other."

Now, if I were thinking clearly, I would've run him over with the forklift, and/or have said, "No thank you." Instead, I stared into his beautiful brown eyes and got lost for a moment and said, "I agree."

It's not that I was lonely or desperate, but I had been day-dreaming about Cameron for a while now. I often fantasized about running my fingers through his wavy chestnut hair or how his warm, firm chest would feel against me or how he would look wearing a suit of armor, galloping his horse across a wide field of green grass in order to save me from a pack of wild animals or a band of ruffians.

I should probably clarify…

Before I took the job at Boltz Hardware, I was a best-selling author. Not bragging- just stating a fact. I'd like to think my books were bestsellers because of the great writing and wonderful character arcs but I'm pretty sure it was because of the sex. People like to read about sex and I'm super gifted at writing *those* kinds of scenes.

I got so tired of churning out the same old bodice-rippers every six months, and I desperately needed a change of pace, so I stopped the grind (pun intended) and I took a job working with my friend, Lacy, at the hardware store.

Other than writing, my passion always ran toward home repair: There was nothing like the smell of warm, burning pitch as I'd cut through a piece of lumber. And the satisfaction I felt after I tiled a kitchen floor or glazed a set of windows was so fulfilling that I wanted to do it over and over again.

I couldn't give up on the writing entirely because I still loved the creative process, but I wanted to write what I wanted to write- not what everyone expected me to write. Like my new novel: It's about a young princess who lived in a castle with her father.

The princess is snatched by a dragon -who really isn't a dragon but is a former king who had a spell cast upon him by an evil sorcerer. Kind of a Beauty and the Beast meets The Hobbit story, and since Cameron was usually on my mind, he inadvertently became one of the characters in my book; thus the fantasy with the suit of armor and the horses. But I digress...

The reality was that Cameron and I would meet in the lumber department inventory room and we'd "talk" about the various wood grades or the massive number of light bulb to light fixture combinations available to the consumer. Always a lively, very sweaty, conversation. We shared a lot of common interests: Grout, electrical conduits, halfpenny nails, general home repair, sex…

I convinced myself that I had finally found my very own Prince Charming. What I found instead was a little white fluffy rabbit.

Let me explain…

I just sat down in the break room across from Lacy and took my first sip of coffee when Scott, the assistant manager, plopped a cage containing a white, fluffy rabbit on the table in front of me. "Rebecca, you can't have livestock in the building. Company policy."

Sidebar here: Why would Scott give me the rabbit if they're banned from the building? It's not like I gave it to myself or carried it into the break room.

Lacy flipped Scott off as soon as his back was turned and gave me an inquisitive look. "Do you think the rabbit's from *him*?" I assumed she meant Cameron.

"I don't know," I said and took the furry bundle out of the cage. I lifted it up so that we were nose to nose. "I guess it's possible. It has been a month."

"A very busy month," she said with a glint in her eye.

I knew what she meant.

Lacy ripped the accompanying note off of the cage and opened it. Her countenance dropped immediately. I snatched it from her.

The note was definitely not what I had expected. The bastard used a sweet, furry, innocent little rabbit to break up with me.

Lacy squeezed my hand and gave me a supportive smile. "I could tell you that you're way better off without him -which you are- but I won't."

"Thanks." She was right, and I knew I was better off without him, but that didn't make it any easier. As far as men went, I was fairly happy with Cameron but I didn't think I was in love with him, and I knew I wouldn't be even if we gave it a year. I didn't want to call things off with him because -let's face it- it was nice to have someone call me once in a while and I loved it when he just held me. Whatever this was between us, it hurt like hell to have it suddenly ripped from me.

In his note, Cameron cited me being "emotionally unavailable" as one of the reasons it didn't work out between us. To be fair, I thought love was some sort of illusion, only realized on TV or in romance novels. Gauging my previous success as a novelist, others saw that illusion of love in my books as well, so I figured I had to have some grasp of the concept. Apparently not.

The closest thing I had ever seen that could be described as actual love was Lacy and her fiancé, Tom. The way they looked at, and cared for each other, I had no doubt that love was what they had. Before them, I'd never seen the effect of love in person.

Scott broke me out of my rumination with a loud burp. "By the way, management wants the Christmas stuff set up by Friday."

"It's September," Lacy stated with obvious disdain.

"And…we just got the soap for the Bubbles and Bullets display. You need to set that up."

Bubbles and Bullets; two things that would not normally fit together. Remember, I live in Martinsburg, West Virginia… Small town. Known mainly for its Civil War history and the most gorgeous autumn you will ever see anywhere else on the planet. According to the Berkeley County Historical Society, lots of famous people passed through here; not many of them stayed, but I loved it. I admit, the place is a bit quirky, but that's part of its charm.

While in the midst of my *literary crisis* Lacy (who had recently followed her fiancé to Martinsburg) called and told me I had a job at the hardware store if I wanted one. Days later, I was driving across the country on Route 66.

Scott burped again. "Your break is over…Both of you."

Still annoyed by Cameron's note, I glared up at him. "Yes, we know. Give us a minute." I looked at the clock. Cameron was a creature of habit and, although we didn't date for long, I knew exactly where he'd be. I grabbed the rabbit and headed for the men's bathroom.

He was just zipping his fly when I burst through the door. He didn't even flinch. "You got the rabbit?"

"Yes." I looked at the cute little bunny and scowled. "You couldn't have done this face to face?"

"I tried."

"When?"

He soaped up his hands and ran them under the faucet. "Last week, when I said we needed to stop seeing each other."

I shook my head in confusion. "You weren't very clear."

"I said, 'Rebecca, we need to stop seeing each other.'"

"But then you kissed me."

"And thus, the rabbit." He took a deep breath and exhaled. My eyes were becoming hot with tears as I imagined my head on his chest, listening to his steady heartbeat in the early morning while he slept. "Listen, Becky, you are a great person but…" He chose that moment to turn on the hand dryer.

I couldn't hear a thing he was saying. He continued to talk just under the level of the noise. "What?"

The dryer shut off and he smiled awkwardly. "I said…" And it was on with the dryer again. I took the hint and deposited the cute little rabbit into his very dry hands. I adjusted my leather tool belt and crashed through the bathroom door, back into the lumber department where things made sense.

While I was contemplating taking the rabbit back -it was a gift after all- a nice married couple joined me at the lumber counter. They looked to be slightly younger than me and I wanted to dislike them immediately for the simple fact that they looked happy. They were at the hardware store together, and that in itself was a sign of a strong, if not tolerant, relationship.

The man placed several yellow paint swatches in front of me. "I'm trying to choose a color that falls between the primrose and the buttercup." As I mentioned before, I worked in LUMBER…not paint so I was confused as to why he was asking me for help.

His wife didn't look happy. "Mike, they're all the same color. Why do you always do this?" Then she looked at me, practically forcing me to choose a side in their domestic dispute. "Tell him they're all the same color."

Mike was getting frustrated. "Nina, just give me a minute."

I tried to remain neutral. "This isn't the paint department, this is lumber." Without looking, I pointed to the sign directly above me. They both gave me the same odd look and I glanced up. To my complete shock, I was in fact in the paint department. Perfect. I'd absently gone to the wrong counter in my distress over the events of the morning. I picked up the intercom. "Joe, you have customers waiting."

Afraid to leave the counter for fear of looking even *stupider* than I felt, I glanced at the paint swatches before me. "Actually, they're all quite different." I had chosen my side. "The primrose is a bit warmer."

Mike smiled. "The buttercup has more blue." I nodded at his observation.

Nina was nearly beside herself. "Seriously, people. Yellow is yellow." She looked at Mike and then locked eyes with me in the hope that her point would somehow, suddenly get through, but it just made things awkward.

I often used the underappreciated *non-sequitur* when finding myself in a situation that was uncomfortable. They were so blatantly obvious that the shock of using one would usually hit the reset button on any awkward conversation. I went for it. I looked directly at Nina and tried my best to own it. "Your husband looks like the type of guy who buys you flowers."

After her initial confusion had passed, Nina nodded and smiled sweetly at him. "He does. He's pretty great, actually."

I smiled at my success. "You're a lucky one. A man who buys you anything is a keeper." I caught a glimpse of Cameron walking across one of the aisles- carrying the rabbit. "Well, other than livestock. That's not such a great gift."

She shrugged. "I suppose it depends on where you grew up."

Chapter 2

I grew up all over the world. My mom and I lived in Kenya until I was four. She worked as an AIDS-trained community health nurse at Nazareth Mission Hospital. Before that, she worked as a nurse for the UN.

At one point, the political climate in Kenya changed severely, and it was suggested, very strongly, that we should head back to the States- immediately. So we did.

My mom couldn't find a job right away at a hospital but instead, got hired as a traveling nurse; so as a result, we moved around a lot. Between the ages of four and six, I lived in almost every state in the U.S. and attended twice as many daycares. Most of the hospitals she worked at graciously provided childcare for the staff so consequentially, I pretty much grew up in a hospital. I was able to make friends quickly, but I always knew I'd be leaving them in a week or two, so I never really got very close to anyone.

She finally got a steady job in Santa Barbara, California, by the time I was six, and my daily routine from then on consisted of walking the three blocks to and from my school to the hospital where I would stop at the cafeteria, grab a snack and give my mom the required call from the cafeteria phone. I didn't want to be stuck in the daycare all day so I'd wander the juvenile cancer treatment floor in search of friends. The nurses didn't seem to mind.

Another sidebar here: What kind of mother lets her six-year-old child wander alone through the halls of a hospital?

I'd always been a bit envious of those kids in the cancer wing because they always had a lot of one-on-one attention, and they had the coolest toys. I remember being super excited over the Lincoln-Logs. We would make the best log cabins and, build blanket forts to cover them.

Every day, I'd see entire families come to the hospital to visit my new friends. I loved watching the families. I wished I had one. Some families were more boisterous than others, but I always found myself watching the dads. They were so interesting to me and I liked the bass in their voices- so different from the sound of my mother's. It was during that first year in Santa Barbara, that I became curious about who my father was.

When I asked my mom about my dad, she told me that I didn't have a father and that I was the happy product of a sperm bank and proceeded to explain to me how I was made without a daddy. I was six…

Imagine my Kindergarten teacher's surprise when, during Show and Tell, I emphatically claimed to be, "just like Baby Jesus because my mom got pregnant without having sex, too!" Before I left school, the teacher used a giant safety pin to attach a note, addressed to my mother, to my shirt. My mother was less than ecstatic when she read the note.

As I grew older, the nurses would see me walking down the hall and would hand me a book directing me to a private room or the large activity room. I was a pretty good reader and sometimes, I would get bored and make up my own stories.

As a result, I made a lot of friends but the kids weren't there for long. Some would be released to go home with their parents; others would go home to be with God. In my child-like mind I thought they were leaving me, rejecting me; which of course they weren't. And I began to learn how to protect myself from that perceived rejection. And thus, my introduction to the short-lived, rejection-proof relationship was formed at an early age. My friendships lasted as long as my mother's job at the hospital did, and I became the queen of the short-lived relationship – romantic or otherwise.

My relationship with Cameron was no exception; in a way, he left me too. Or maybe I left him before he had a chance to. I don't know.

To be honest, I think the reason our breakup affected me so much more than it should have was that I had projected an unrealistic fantasy on Cameron for years before we actually dated. When our relationship finally became a reality, and he didn't live up to those ridiculous expectations, I was disappointed.

He wasn't a knight in shining armor or a fairy tale prince. No one could live up to that standard. It just wasn't realistic. Cameron wasn't a bastard…he was just a guy.

Oddly, it was his gift of that rabbit that knocked me over the head and finally helped me clue into my unhealthy habit of creating ridiculous fantasies of fairy-tale love, about the men I dated and the things I longed to have: A real father, a perfect husband, maybe children and a house with a white picket fence. That's just too much pressure to put on anyone. I'd run, too. I didn't have an actual coherent train of thought that started with "Hey, there's this super cute rabbit in my hand." and ended with "Wow, I totally projected my unrealistic fantasy world on Cameron." But somehow, in the middle of everything, I had an epiphany.

Life could never be the way I wanted it to be…not exactly anyway. But nothing would change if I didn't get a grip and start living in the present. I knew I couldn't change the circumstances of my past, but I could change my perception of the future. I knew I could condition myself to live in reality and to stop trying to fill the holes in my life I thought I had, with the things I thought I needed.

I met Lacy in the break room later that day and recounted my epiphany about the rabbit and the unrealistic fantasy world I was living in.

"You need to help me come up with a plan to make me be less emotionally unavailable for future relationships."

She looked at me sideways. "I have no idea how to help you with that."

My eyes pleaded with her.

She slurped on her juice box. She loved those things. "Ok...Umm...Why do you think you're that way?"

"No idea."

She took a deep breath. "Maybe you need to figure out *why* your heart is so protected in order to figure out *what* to change?"

She was a very smart woman. "To go in with an open heart...That's the part I'm really not sure how to do."

She looked at me blankly. "What are you talking about?"

"I don't think I know how to love anyone."

Lacy laughed at me. "Of course, you know how to love. You are one of the most caring people I know."

I guess what she said made sense. I had never really felt like I was shut off to others and I did like people. Sure, I didn't have a lot of friends but in my opinion, a person only needs one or two great friends. It's hard to spend any quality time with more than that.

Especially being a writer.

I spend hours a day alone writing or thinking about my characters, and until I finish the book I'm obsessed with it. I have no time for a lot of friends because the *friends* occupying my mind are the characters in my books. And *they* aren't emotionally unavailable so how can I be if I created them?

But the truth was, I felt safe opening the hearts of my characters because ultimately, they weren't real and they couldn't get hurt. I could.

"How would I even know if it was love or not? Seriously, how do people know if they are in love?"

She smiled a knowing smile, "Trust me. When you've found him, you'll know." She saw my trepidation and took a deep breath. "I promise. You'll know it when it happens. You just haven't found the right guy, yet."

"How do you know? What if I have and I messed it up? I mean, I've dated plenty of guys."

She looked directly into my eyes and I knew she believed what she said. "You will find someone to love and he will love you back. Of that, I have no doubt."

I just wished I believed her as well.

Chapter 3

That evening when I got home, I cried broken dreams into my throw pillow, until the BLOOP of a Skype call grabbed my attention. I wiped my face and answered the call. It was my mother, Vicki. I took a deep breath and smiled bravely.

With a click, my mom's face appeared on the screen. "Hello, Rebecca." Her white face and overly dark hair were a bit of a shock, and I don't think I'm out of line when I say that some people of a certain age should avoid wearing bikinis.

"Hello, Mom." I noticed palm trees swaying behind her against a vibrant blue sky and realized that she was not at her home in Oregon. "Where are you?"

"Mozambique," she said as if it were the most natural thing for her to be in Africa.

Her pasty white abdomen was blinding me. "You should really cover up a bit. Don't ya think?"

"Oh, honey. Don't be such a prude." Mercifully, she covered herself up. "Why are your eyes all bloodshot?"

"My boyfriend broke up with me." The impending floodgate of emotion was now stuck in my throat. I glanced at the note from Cameron.

"He thinks I'm emotionally unavailable."

"You did have trouble making friends in the first grade." I never quite understood why I continued to share things with her. Habit, I suppose. Somehow, I always felt worse after talking with my mother.

She took a loud sip of her umbrella drink. "Redecorating again?"

At that moment, I realized where I learned the art of being emotionally unavailable: My mother.

I turned and looked at the wall behind me. (I might have gotten distracted before I finished painting it.) But "Yeah," was all I could get out. The epic revelation that I had learned to be emotionally stunted from my mother should have made me angry but it actually gave me a great sense of relief. Nurture NOT nature. I wasn't doomed.

A knock at the front door interrupted our conversation.

I was hoping it was Cameron, ready to beg my forgiveness, on his knees – so he was at the right level for me to kick him in the teeth- but alas, it was a FedEx guy.

"Sign here," he said without much emotion. I did, and he was gone.

I stood at the door a moment longer and then opened the FedEx package. Inside was a pinkish envelope with the most beautiful handwriting I had seen from anyone in this century. The letter inside was written in the same languid hand as the envelope.

"Rebecca?" I was brought back to the present, upon hearing my mother call me from the other side of the world. Removing the colorful straw from her mouth my mom nodded toward the envelope. "What did you get?"

I shushed her with a wave of my hand while I read the note.

> *Rebecca,*
>
> *I would like to inform you that your father, James McDermott, may have had a bit of a heart attack recently. I know you've never met him but I thought now might be a good time for you to come to Scotland so the two of you could have a chat in the*

event that he may turn up deceased at some point.

Yours, Beatrice- Estate Manager,
for Laird McDermott, Baron of
Lairsach, Scottish Highlands.

I was beyond confused. I checked the outside of the FedEx envelope one more time just to make certain that my name was actually written on the front- it was. I waved the letter at my mother. "Who is James McDermott?"

"Oh, that's interesting." She stared blankly at me.

If I could have grabbed her by her neck through the computer screen, I would have. "Who. Is. He?"

"James McDermott? He's your father," she said, nonchalantly taking another loud sip of her stupid umbrella drink.

Ok…That was unexpected. "I don't have a father."

"Everybody has a father."

"Yes, but you know what I mean."

"Well, about that."

The silence was deafening.

"Wait, you mean, you had actual sex with him?" The minute those words flew from my mouth I regretted saying them.

"Yes, Rebecca. Actual sex."

"So, I didn't come from a test tube?

"No."

"And you didn't think that was important information for me to have?"

"Not at the time."

I paced back and forth in front of the multi-colored wall. "Sperm bank, Mom?" I thought I was going to be sick. My whole life was a lie. Well, the dad part anyway- I was fairly certain that she was still my mother. But why not tell me the truth? Or at the least make up a better lie than *sperm bank*.

"You could have told me that my father was protesting apartheid in South Africa and was shot while handing out leaflets. Or, since you were lying to me anyway how about, 'Hey little six-year-old Rebecca, your dad died saving a pod of orcas. He was a freakin' hero.'"

"Come on. Saving orcas wasn't even a thing back then."

"You're missing the point."

She set her drink on the table next to her. "The truth?"

"That would be nice."

With a deep breath, she began. "Your father and I met at a Country Club in Kenya, while I was working as a nurse for the UN. He was a Second Lieutenant in the British Army. Anyway, the Army transferred him somewhere..."

"He's British?"

"Scottish."

"I'm Scottish?"

"Only Half."

I couldn't breathe. I was absolutely stunned. I couldn't believe that I actually had a father. A real father, not one I fabricated in my mind.

My mother's voice snapped me out of it. "You alright?"

"Not remotely." I sat down in front of the screen and checked the time. "I need to go to work." She nodded and chomped on the pineapple impaled by the sharp end of her drink umbrella. I shut the computer and remembered why it had been over seven months since I had spoken to my mother.

Chapter 4

As I rode my bike the four miles to work the next morning, I couldn't help but re-examine my entire existence. I was raised by a mother who had lied to me my entire life. Part of me wanted to believe that she only wanted to protect me. The rest of me knew she was protecting herself.

The thing that really bothered me was that thirty years of my life had gone by and my relationship with my father was wasted because my mom was too self-absorbed to contact him earlier. I could never get those years back. I was pissed. I pedaled my bike like my very life depended on it and with all of the extra adrenaline coursing through my body from the anger and a near accident, I arrived at work 20 minutes early. I decided to write a bit in my notebook while I waited for my shift to begin.

I dug around in my backpack for my notebook, but it was gone. After searching to no avail, I looked up to see Lacy walking toward me, waving the notebook gleefully over her head.

Lacy is one of those "beautiful on the inside, beautiful on the outside" kind of woman. When she laughs, she laughs with her entire being. It is very contagious and I can't help laughing as well. Sometimes, I'm not sure if I'm laughing at her or with her but her good-nature always puts me in a good mood. Well, except for today. "Why do you have my notebook?"

"Because I wanted to read it."

"It's not finished."

"Yes, I know. It's actually really good, though." And then she read some of it out loud. I could've killed her. *Once upon a time there lived a beautiful princess with hair the color of a sunset. Her name was Abigail. Abigail lived with her father, the king, in a castle on top of a beautiful hill, covered with red poppies and purple heather.*

I snatched the notebook out of her hand. "Yeah. Fantasy trumps reality, every time." I had no aspirations of being the next Great American Novelist but I wanted to write one more novel, on my own terms. I wanted to see if I could be successful writing something that I could be proud of. I shoved the notebook deep into my backpack. "If you touch this again before I'm done..."

"And when will that be? You're in the same place you were a month ago." She threw me a WTF glance over her shoulder. "I thought you were a writer."

I shrugged. "I'm just not inspired."

"Whatever." Lacy smirked and grabbed the Homefinder Magazine off the table. She pointed to the photo of a very small, very run-down house that I had circled the other day in red marker. "This house again?"

"Yeah. It's been on the market forever." I took a long look at the photo.

Lacy lifted her eyebrow in disgust.

"It's a fixer-upper." I scowled.

"Looks like a meth lab."

I took a closer look and nodded. "That's quite possible." I sighed with resignation. "I just want a place of my own. I'm so tired of renting." I wanted to finally belong somewhere and I thought the best way to do that would be to put down some roots. What better way to put down roots than to get into debt with a house of my own?

It was a slow morning at work and since we had finished setting up the Christmas decorations in record time yesterday, Lacy and I were tasked with the duty of assembling sheds. Give me a saw or a drill and I am a happy woman.

I filled Lacy in on the details of my parentage as we completed the assembly of the sheds. "All these years and you never knew?" We lifted one of the pre-assembled walls onto a pallet and Lacy braced it with an angled 2x4.

I let go of the wall and grabbed my drill. I pressed it firmly into the head of the screw so I didn't strip it. "Nope. Mother of the year." The screw slid into the wall like butter.

"So, are you going?" She asked.

"To Scotland?"

"Durr." Lacy grabbed her drill and advanced a screw into the wood.

"I don't want to waste a bunch of money on a flight and hotel just to be rejected by my *father*. He didn't even write me that letter himself. It was from some woman."

"Maybe he had her write it. Those rich guys never do anything for themselves. Wait. Is he rich?"

I shrugged.

"You didn't Google him?"

"No. I'm not ready yet."

"You know, that's probably a good idea. Make your own judgments about him." She got quiet and I saw her mind spinning. Lacy lost her father last year to cancer and had barely made it to him before he passed. They weren't on the best of terms but she was very thankful she decided to go. "You have to go see him. Immediately…this week!" Her eyes locked onto mine.

I drove a final screw into the wall. "I don't think I could deal with another rejection just now."

She caught my eye like she meant business. "I'd be so mad at myself if I knew my dad was alive and I never made the effort to meet him. If he dies, you'll never forgive yourself."

On cue, a father and daughter duo entered the store laughing and holding hands. I stared at them for a long time. It was a thing of beauty, really.

"What the heck am I supposed to say to him? 'Hey... dad...sorry you had a heart attack. Can you try to hold off on dying for a bit while I get to know you?'"

"Sure you could say that or, you could lead with, 'Hi, I'm Rebecca. I am of your loins.'" Lacy checked the sturdiness of the four walls.

"Yeah. I think I'll say that...."

"Does that mean you're going?" She smiled her smile.

I laughed. "I'll think about it. If I do go...and I'm not saying that I will, should I give him a head's up or should I just show up? I think I should just show up. That's not weird or anything."

"Totally weird. But if it'll take the pressure off, just show up." Lacy had a way of simplifying things.

"I agree. It might be a bit strange to pop in on him out of nowhere but if I did that, at least I'd have the option to bail if I decided not to see him." We headed back inside and I thought about what Lacy said. I guess I really would be mad at myself if I wasted time and when I finally got around to going to Scotland, my bio-dad was dead. "Scottish? Never guessed that I was Scottish. I guess that explains the red hair."

"Be happy you aren't Irish. There's a whole shit-load of issues associated with them."

"Aren't they pretty much the same thing? I mean, I realize they're different countries but..."

"No! And don't say that to anyone over there. You might get skewered or something. Lots of empty land to bury you in...Your body wouldn't be found for decades."

"Excellent."

"Gotta love those sexy men in kilts, though. Take some pictures."

"You're engaged."

Lacy scrunched up her face. "Get a grip. I only asked you to take some pictures, not bring one home for me."

I changed my mind about going to Scotland at least seven times before I headed home and realized that for the first time in my life, I felt like I was totally alone. I had no boyfriend, which was probably a good thing. My writing career was on hold. I wasn't planning on talking to my mom for at least a year this time around and although I had a real father I had no idea what he would do when I showed up on his doorstep. I still had Lacy, of course, but she would be married soon, and I knew things would never be the same again.

It's never good to drown one's sorrows in alcohol, but I decided to succumb just this once. The only alcohol I had in my house at that moment was an unopened pint of corn whiskey (otherwise known as moonshine- a gift from my friends at Black Draft Distillery) and I didn't really think things through before I took my first of many shots. This was 100 proof, I might add.

You can probably see where this is going...

I ordered way too much Chinese food for delivery and once it arrived; I ate, drank some more moonshine, watched part of the Colin Firth version of Pride and Prejudice then swapped it out in favor of Braveheart. I drank some more and, re-read the letter from Beatrice regarding my *father*. Things got a bit fuzzy after that.

I remember wondering how I would fit into this new culture with its wonderful history and traditions. I remember getting on the computer, and I vaguely remember looking at rental cars and flights to Scotland, and then I fell asleep… Well, passed out would probably be more accurate.

When I woke up the next morning, I had a really bad headache, blurry blood-shot eyes, cotton mouth and a crick in my neck from the couch. I grabbed some water and ibuprofen and decided then and there, that it was time I took charge of my life instead of waiting for someone else to do it for me.

I had nothing to lose by going to Scotland but I had no idea how my father would react to me. Would he hate me? Would he ignore me? Would my sudden appearance give him another heart-attack? I had heard that the Highlanders of Scotland were well…kind of like the Mountain People of the Ozarks: Gun crazy and crazy for blood. Braveheart was pretty intense. I had no idea what I was going to find when I showed up there.

I checked my email before I got serious about looking at flights and saw several emails from Priceline and eBay congratulating me on my recent purchases.

Much to my surprise, I had *drunk-bought* an airplane ticket to Glasgow- leaving tonight- and I bought a convertible as well. It's a good thing I had a current passport.

I figured that since I had the car and non-refundable airplane tickets – for a three-month stay I might add- I should probably rent a house of some sort just in case I decided to avoid my father. I booked a cute, little cottage right outside of the quaint town of Newtonmore.

The sober me decided that the drunk me could NEVER come out to play again- she was NOT a cheap date.

Chapter 5

As my flight began its final descent into Glasgow Airport, the seatbelt symbol above my head *binged* on and the stewardess gave her customary speech. "Your Captain has turned on the fasten seatbelt sign. Please return to your seats as we are preparing for our final descent into the Glasgow International Airport. Return your tray tables and chair backs to their locked and upright position and turn off all electronic devices and securely stow your belongings under the seat in front of you."

I turned to the man sitting next to me in First Class (my impulse-buying, drunken self, spared no expense) and smiled broadly at him. He was a burly, kind-looking fellow in his mid-fifties. His Armani suit, Bottega Veneta dress shoes, and Breitling watch were a drastic contradiction to his receding hairline and severe case of myopia.

"You are so great. It was very helpful to have someone to talk to on occasion, you know, to pass the time." I looked seriously at the man who was nodding in agreement. "You aren't a therapist are you?"

"Aye," he said and I giggled nervously.

"Oh, well then, I guess we should probably introduce ourselves in case you need to bill me. I'm Rebecca. Nice to meet you." I thrust out my hand in friendship. The man received the gesture.

"Niles. You could talk the ears off a sow, Lass. But you did help pass the time and for that, I am grateful." I smiled back in mortification but his Scottish burr was awesome so that took the edge off.

He patted my hand. "A wee word of advice if ye dunna mind?"

I laughed nervously. "Sure. It's the least I can do."

"Sometimes, it's better to be a doer rather than a talker. You are obviously the latter. Jump in with your whole being and see where it takes you. Don't stop to think about it first."

*   *   *

After clearing customs with no trouble, I looked around at the sea of total strangers before me and smiled. A very loud group of hairy-legged kilted men carrying bagpipes and pulling suitcases caught my attention. I laughed out loud and then looked around to see if I had offended anyone. The coast was clear.

I took a few pictures of the mass of kilted humanity with my phone and sent the photos to Lacy. She'd love me forever.

I was in such a daze when I left the U.S. that I never actually told her I was leaving. When I finally remembered, I emailed her from the airplane. I hadn't intentionally withheld the trip from her. To be honest, if I had stopped to think about any of this I might not have gone through with it. But there was no turning back now.

When I sobered up the morning after my impulse-buy, I contacted the dealer who sold me the car on e-Bay. He assured me that someone would be waiting for me with the car as I exited the plane. I looked from sign to sign and found my name being held by a jovial, tweed-clad gentleman. He helped me gather my luggage and ushered me outside to my cute little red car. He handed me the keys and paperwork without ceremony and left me with a nod and a smile and a full tank of gas.

As usual, I packed way more for the trip than any one person could possibly need, and being hung-over, I really didn't think things through. The trunk of the car (or boot, apparently) was so tiny, that it disappeared when I raised the convertible top. After I assessed the lack of adequate space and shoved my various smaller bags behind the seats, I proceeded to wrestle my extra-large suitcase into the passenger seat. It weighed more than a small adult and I had to hook the seatbelt around the luggage to get the car to stop beeping at me.

After I got the car loaded, I situated myself in the driver's seat- which was on the WRONG side of the car. I never thought about the whole "shifting with the left hand" thing either before I bought it…Hell, I didn't even remember buying the car in the first place, but here I was; in my very own convertible…In Scotland. I sure hope it didn't rain.

I put the car in gear and looked over my right shoulder. Instead of backing up I lurched forward and nearly crashed into the side of a building. I closed my eyes, took a couple of deep breaths and tried again. "You've got this."

Success. I managed to get out of the parking space, but it took me forever to find my way out of the damned airport. I drove around and around that place for forty-five minutes before I found the correct sign for the *carriageway* that would led me north.

* * *

I found myself driving a bit on the slow side as I attempted to navigate the narrow, curvy roads of the Scottish countryside--sometimes on the correct side of the road, sometimes not. Although, who really knew? There were no lines dividing most of the roads anyway and I had no way of knowing if I were on a one-way road or not. On some of the roads, there were random arrows pointing into and out of my side of the road but I didn't have any idea what they meant.

In the midst of my trauma and uncertainty, I did manage to sneak the occasional glance at the lush, green, rugged hills and the beautiful blue sky; when I wasn't busy white-knuckling the steering wheel. The scenery was nothing like I had ever seen. Sure, I had seen photographs before but I had no idea how small and insignificant I would feel until I was surrounded by the unadulterated beauty and unending vastness of the Scottish Highlands.

Ruining my perfect mood, a man in the car behind me rudely laid on his horn and nearly hit me from behind. The driver glared at me as he passed – on a blind corner I might add- and yelled something that sounded like English but I wasn't sure.

"What is wrong with you people?", I yelled after him.

The very posh sounding woman on my GPS interrupted my tirade. "Turn right in 200 meters." I glanced down at the map on my phone and when I looked up, I was face to face with a huge, hairy, horned beast of some kind chewing a wad of grass in the middle of the road. I screamed and swerved to miss it. I skidded through the loose dirt of the shoulder and overcorrected the car. There was nothing I could do as I flew across to the opposite side of the road and crashed headlong into a stack of beehives. Those things must've contained at least a million bees. They were very irritated and engulfed me immediately.

I jumped out of the car and high-tailed it away from the bees flailing my arms spastically. My body was on fire- the pain wouldn't stop. I couldn't think. All I could do was scream and run around like a crazy person. Bees clung to my clothing, so I stripped them off piece by piece, tossing them as far away from me as they would go. They were clothes, so they didn't go very far.

Just as I was about to remove my bra, I found myself being doused by freezing cold, green, slimy water. I stopped dead in my tracks. I gagged on my newly matted, algae-covered hair, most of which was stuck to my face or lodged in my mouth and for a split-second, I had forgotten about the bees.

I turned and found myself face to face with the most handsomely rugged, dark-haired man I had ever seen.

"You alright?" If love-at-first-sight were a thing, this would have been it. He was gorgeous, but that voice? That accent. Damn. It may have been more of a British accent than a Scottish one, but what did I know? My understanding of Scotland was pretty much limited to watching *Braveheart* and eating oatmeal…and I did catch the end of *Local Hero* on the airplane.

"Are you crazy? That's cold!"

"Am I crazy? I'm not the one runnin' 'round Scotland with her knickers on. Am I?" It took me a minute to realize that I was standing in the middle of nowhere -mostly naked- and covered in algae. I cleared the clumps of hair from my face the best I could and smiled at his kindness.

His crisp, green eyes nearly popped out of his head at the sight of me. "Bloody hell!" I don't know if he was expecting to rescue a fair maiden, but based on his reaction, he realized that he had just rescued a horrible beast.

I put my hand to my face, which felt swollen in places. My hands were swollen and my eyes were getting harder to keep open as well. After he concluded that I was human, he smiled warmly, staring at my face and body with pity. I was both embarrassed and offended at the same time.

"You aren't allergic to bees, are you?" The man stepped so close to me that I could feel his very warm breath on my bare skin.

I shrugged. "Not that I know of but I've never been stung this many times before."

The man looked really concerned and he reached toward my lip. "Hold still a minute."

I reeled back in panic and slapped him –unintentionally- across the face. "What?! Ohmygosh get it off!"

He grabbed both of my flailing hands firmly in his very warm and very strong hands and spoke quietly and calmly. "Calm down, Luv. It's just a stinger." He looked deep into my soul with a gentle forcefulness that took my breath away. "May I?"

I nodded in agreement. Damn, this guy was beautiful. He actually looked like he was glowing, but I think it may have been the green sludge that was still coating my eyeballs...

I watched him reach slowly toward my swollen upper lip to remove the stinger. He gently passed his finger over my lip to remove any leftover residue that may have been left behind from the stinger and I felt a rush of anticipation course through my body.

"Your lips are very soft." He leaned toward me as though he were planning to kiss me, and I leaned in too, but instead of planting one on me, he held up the stinger for my review. Awkward...

He gently tucked a lock of hair behind my ear and removed a second stinger from my cheek.

I took a cursory glance at my shins. "Do you think there could be...more...on my body?"

"I don't know. Would you like me to look?"

Hell yes, I did. I didn't want those things in there any longer than was necessary. They freakin' hurt. I nodded again. "Absolutely."

Taking more time than he probably needed, the man gave my body a thorough examination being careful not to miss an inch of my flesh. I can't say I minded much. I was in heaven–aside from the searing pain coursing through my body in waves. His touch was electric.

He completed his examination by brushing the hair from my left shoulder to my right. "Hold still." He bent his head closer to my neck. His breath was warm on my chilled skin. And then it was over. He—and his adorable half-smile—showed me a final stinger. "That should do it."

With a surge of relief, I launched myself into his arms. "Thank you!"

"You are very welcome, Luv."

"You're so warm." I didn't realize how cold I was. I pressed myself further into his warmth.

He chuckled and hugged me back. "Why thank you… um…What's your name?"

Oh wonderful, I'd just thrown myself into the arms of a total stranger. I pulled back in mortification and…holy shit! I was still unclothed. I was beyond embarrassed. "I'm Becca… Becky…Rebecca."

He laughed good-naturedly. "I'll just take my pick, then?"

I nodded.

He stepped away from me and gathered my clothes.

I took them and shook out each item with fervor hoping that there weren't any stray stingers remaining.

"Alright, Becca. I'm Gavin. Pleased to meet you on this fine Scottish morning." He thrust out his hand and I took it to shake it but instead he kissed the back of it. I looked around to see if we were being filmed. Someone HAD to be punking me because this guy could not be for real. He couldn't be. No one who was *that* good looking could be that sweet. "Where were you headed before you…?" He looked toward my car.

"Some place near Newtonmore." I followed Gavin's gaze toward my car, which was still active with bees. "The address is on my phone…"

Gavin touched my hand lightly and met my gaze with assurance. "I'll be right back." He zipped up his jacket and spoke to me with a backward glance up and down my body. "You may want to get dressed." He shoved his helmet over his head and jogged toward my car.

Shit. I still wasn't dressed. He was so distracting. Now I really wondered what he thought of me. I took stock of my body as I replaced my clothes. I didn't look too bad–other than the bee stings, that is. I probably had twenty to thirty sting marks on my front and probably the same amount on my back. Thank God I had been working out regularly over the past year. I shook my head at this less than awesome beginning to my new life. "The best-looking guy you've ever seen in your life and you are in your *knickers* the whole time," I mumbled. I had barely finished slipping on my shoes when Gavin returned.

Being *gallant* he handed me my purse, car keys and phone with a royal bow, "Your belongings, my Lady."

I noticed a large welt growing on the top of his hand. "Oh no, you've been stung." I grabbed his hand and without thinking, skimmed my finger gently over the welt. "You aren't allergic are you?"

Gavin smiled oddly at my concern and shook his head. "No, but you're actually starting to swell badly. We need to get you to a chemist."

"What about my car?"

Gavin seemed amused. "I don't think anyone'll touch it. I'll call for a tow after we get you taken care of." He hopped on the back of his bike and handed me his extra helmet. "Hop on."

I was torn between guarding my car and its contents and getting medical attention but in the end, I opted for the wiser of the two choices and climbed on behind Gavin. I slung my purse across my body, and in a last effort of protecting my car, I pressed the automatic lock button on my fob before dropping my keys into my massive purse. My convertible flashed and beeped in obedience. I smiled sheepishly at Gavin who was still smirking at me.

"Helmet," was all he said, and I obeyed.

Chapter 6

My face was still on fire as I walked out of Boot's drug-store covered in pink calamine lotion and wearing my new hot pink velour sweat suit. (It was the only color they had.) I twisted off the top of a bottle of antihistamine -which also happened to be pink- and I choked down half of it.

Gavin laughed and took his time looking me up and down. "You fancy the color pink, then?"

I did like the color pink but none of this was intentional. I smirked and gulped back half of the bottle of the bright pink liquid.

"You may want to take it easy with that." Gavin nodded at the bottle in my hand.

I took another swig, and wiped my face with the sleeve of my sweat suit. "It's okay. My mom's a nurse." Like that legitimized my behavior? People say stuff like that all of the time. It makes no sense.

Truth was, I couldn't think particularly straight. Yes, I was in terrible pain, very uncomfortable, and definitely jet-lagged but I wasn't so clueless that I didn't notice Gavin staring at me *that way.* He leaned toward me and gently unstuck a glob of my green-slime hair that was now glued to the dried pink goo on my face. He nodded toward his motorcycle. "We should probably get going."

"Are you sure I shouldn't just call a cab?" I dropped the remaining half bottle of Benadryl into my huge purse. "I don't want you to go out of your way."

Gavin shook his head. "No taxis around here, and I'm going that direction anyway. I'll take you. "

I looked around the sleepy, vacant town and realized that there weren't any options better than this one. And as options went, this wasn't such a bad one. Aside from the fact that Gavin was strong and beautiful, he rode a motorcycle. I loved men who rode motorcycles. But I wasn't entirely without a brain, so before I embarked into the unknown, I snapped a photo of him and texted it to Lacy just in case. I had a feeling this guy wasn't the type who would hurt anyone, but you just never know.

"You alright?"

I was in a new country, I was freezing, I was lost and I was tired and a little scared. I wondered if I should get to a hospital but I was able to breathe just fine and since my mother *was* a nurse, and I grew up in a hospital, I figured the worst was over and I'd be alright just going home. I was really thankful he didn't just leave me alone. I nodded bravely and climbed onto the bike. "I'm great. Thanks again for the ride. You're a real knight in shining armor."

"Aye. That I am." Gavin took off so rapidly that I was forced to wrap my arms tightly around his waist to avoid falling off the back of the bike. I saw him smirk in the side mirror and I clung to him even tighter -more out of enjoyment than out of necessity.

Upon turning a blind corner on the way out of town, we nearly broadsided a taxi. I smacked him on the shoulder but had to smile at his mischievous reflection.

Gavin nodded. "I wasn't sure I was quite ready to exchange you for your phone number."

I glared into the mirror. "How do you know I'd even give you my number?"

He smiled his crooked smile. "How else would you find your car?"

"Touché…" I shrugged and snuggled closer. "If I promise to give you my number, you promise to tell me where the car is going…Just in case you don't call me."

"It's at the Fox and Hen pub."

"Pub?"

"Aye. It's a small town. The pub owner, Ned, is also the mechanic. He's the town's lawyer as well just in case you suffer any legal ramifications for annihilating those hives."

"Good to know."

"And, I'll call you."

He was adorable.

After a while, my brain began to get a bit fuzzy and I relaxed to the point of almost falling asleep a time or two as we rocked gently on the winding roads threading through the beautiful countryside. The pain over my body was beginning to lessen and the swelling on my face and lips felt like it went down. The Benadryl seemed to have done its job, or maybe it was the cold wind hitting my face that numbed it to the point of relief. Either way, I was thankful for the reprieve.

However, the unsettling drop toward the river on the right kept me from relaxing entirely. I couldn't stop myself from thinking about the possibility of plunging off the cliff to our deaths the way Gavin was driving. But the fear held my fatigue at bay for the time being, and I was able to check out the resplendent view.

Low-flying grouse and spotted ptarmigans took their turns escaping the offensive noise of Gavin's motorcycle. Geese squawked overhead and I saw a fair amount of wild Scottish hares hopping from safety to safety. Many of the hills were dotted with white sheep that lazily grazed on the green grass, between clumps of purple heather and red poppies.

Every so often when a hill would give way to a valley, I would catch sight of an old, deteriorating castle crowning the crest of a hill and couldn't help wondering about the people who once inhabited those immense places: The songs they played, the stories they told and the people they loved flashed through my mind like a film on fast-forward. I was more eager than ever to begin writing again.

My mind wandered to my novel and I began to zone out a bit. I usually called that my *writer-zone*. Not very original I admit. Lacy called it my *zombie face* because, according to her, I looked totally lifeless when I zoned out. Either way, I was generally not mentally present in whatever was going on at the time.

As a writer, I often injected various characteristics of my own personality into the characters in my novel. I lived in a contrived fantasy world most of the time anyway, and since I was the one spending the time with the characters, I figured I might as well be a part of it. However, the heroine that I was writing about in my new novel, Abigail, was nothing like me. She was sweet, and fun and innocent; and definitely emotionally available.

If I were the heroine of this novel, I'd probably be covered in mud, cruising down these hills on a mountain bike or on an ATV.

Abigail would be skipping across the green fields; ripe with red poppies, yellow black-eyed Susans and purple thistles.

Abigail's gauzy white dress would flow behind her and curl gently around her ankles *as she stopped to pluck a yellow flower, hidden in the shadow of a large gray stone.*

She climbed onto the stone and looked out over the kingdom as she absently created a necklace and crown out of the flowers she had collected. She sighed and closed her eyes. "I know you are out there, my love. I am waiting."

She shook her head at the silly notion that she was in love with a dream. Since she was a small girl, she had heard his voice. The voice of her true love. She had never seen him, nor did she know what the man looked like but she was certain that she would know him when they met.

She turned at the sound of hoof beats and stood abruptly. A knight on horseback galloped up next to her and, with a flourish, dismounted his steed, removed his helmet and scooped her up into his arms before planting a very firm kiss on her lips.

Abigail was too stunned to do anything but to stare wide-eyed at this man she had only met but the once.

"Abigail, my love, it appears that I have been remiss in my duty to my father, and suddenly, I find myself in desperate need of a wife. "

Abigail's smile faded, and she stared blankly at the misdirected but very handsome man. "I'm sorry, Milord, but was that a proposal? "

The knight took a step back and began again with a cough. "Yes. I see." He took a deep breath, took her hands in his and dropped to his knee. "I am a man of good standing and I think you should become my wife."

Abigail nodded at the knight standing before her and squared her shoulders. " Milord." She curtseyed. "Whilst I am very flattered by your ever so…uh…gallant offer for my hand I fear I must decline."

The man didn't seem to hear her because he slipped a beautiful ring upon her finger and stood to kiss her hand thinking that there would be nothing more to say.

She clenched her jaw and took a calming breath, all the while trying to keep a serene smile on her face. She would have words with her father about this the moment she escaped this very persistent suitor. "But again good sir." She removed the ring and held it out to the knight. "I must beg your pardon and return to my father, the King." To the knight's dismay, Abigail turned and fairly ran toward the castle.

Gavin gunned it around another sharp bend in the road snapping me out of the zone. I gripped him tighter and saw Gavin smile in the side mirror. He was beautiful when he smiled. His approach to getting me closer was kind of adorable so I complied, very willingly, and snuggled into him even closer. If only I could be Abigail and if only Gavin could be the man Abigail knew in her heart to be the love of her life… Crap! I was doing it again.

I stopped myself from pulling Gavin into my fantasy world and smiled at his very real reflection in the side mirror…On a motorcycle…after he LITERALLY rescued me from a swarm of bees. Hmmmm.

Around the next bend, the hills opened up to a lush, green field occupied by a herd of the same hairy beasts I had swerved to miss earlier that morning. The long-haired creatures looked a lot like buffalo, but they also looked like oxen.

"What are they?" I yelled over the noise and pointed toward the offending animals.

"Highland cows."

I shook my head. There was absolutely no way those were cows. The road noise and his accent made things difficult to hear so I thought I ought to clarify. "Cows?"

He nodded. "Aye." As if on cue one of them lifted its head and ground its grass between its molars, seemingly unfazed by the noise of the motorcycle. I guess it looked a little like a cow.

As we rode on, I found myself growing accustomed to the noise of the motorcycle as well as the smell of leather and gasoline. Who knew that leather and gas could be such an amazing combination? I took a deep breath and snuggled, once again, into Gavin's back.

Gavin smiled at our closeness and tucked one of my swollen pink hands under his arm with his free hand as he threaded his way skillfully through the Scottish Highlands. I was amazed at how easily such a small gesture touched my heart. This was new for me. Protection. I closed my eyes and snuggled a little closer.

Chapter 7

Gavin felt her grip tighten and her body relax into him. He smiled and continued on a bit more slowly toward Newtonmore. He wasn't sure what to think of this lass, but he wanted to savor the time he had with her.

He also knew that he was damn curious to see her when she didn't look like the elephant man. He was strangely attracted to her now even with the pink crap all over her and her misshapen face. She was surprising, and Gavin hadn't been surprised by anyone in a long time.

He swore off long-term relationships years ago when his ex-fiancée, Emma, decided that she would rather move back to her home in Finland than marry him and live in Scotland. She said she couldn't handle the weather or the lack of excitement in the Highlands, and Gavin couldn't move away from Scotland because of family obligations, so they were at an impasse. Of course, she never did invite him to come with her to Finland, which was for the best. He wouldn't have gone anyway.

Looking back, Gavin realized that their relationship was safe and familiar but not protective or passionate. There was no fire. Emma recently announced via Facebook, that she had gotten married and that she and her new husband were expecting their first child. Gavin was numb to the news.

He had been numb for a long time- even before they broke up.

Gavin knew he had been sleep-walking through life well before they met and he wasn't overly happy with his current situation either. Choices were made for him over the course of his life, and he felt he had no control over them. He tried to press against it and change his circumstances, but Scotland was a country rooted in history and tradition so, seeing that there was no way out of his predicament, sleepwalking through life seemed to be the only way to survive.

Then, just hours ago, Rebecca catapulted into his life… running around like a deranged mental patient in all of her glory, and suddenly he felt like he was awake for the first time in a decade. She was swollen beyond recognition and could barely function with all of the pain she must've been in and all of the histamines coursing through her very fit body, but something about her intrigued him. Something about her felt like home.

Gavin turned off the main road onto an arterial and slowed down to avoid running into a herd of highland cattle being slowly coaxed across the road by a weather-beaten farmer. Archie smiled warmly and waved a bony hand at Gavin. "Hiya, Gavin."

"Archie." Gavin loosed his grip on her hand and turned around in his seat intending to tell Rebecca that her house was right ahead of them, past the herd of cattle but saw her start to slide off of the seat behind him. He set the kick-stand as quickly as possible but wasn't able to prevent Rebecca from landing on the muddy road.

"I think yer passenger has abandoned ship."

"I think you may be right." Rebecca was sleeping peacefully in the mud in the middle of the street.

Archie took a closer look. "She's pink!"

Rebecca woke briefly to see Gavin and a wrinkled-old-man very near her face. She smiled drunkenly at the two men.

"Up you go." Gavin tried his best to get Rebecca to walk the 200 meters to her cottage under her own strength, but she was far too relaxed, so he heaved her over his shoulder like she weighed nothing. Rebecca grunted something unintelligible and then returned to her antihistamine-induced coma.

Archie patted Gavin on the back in satisfaction. "Well done, lad. That's how we did it in my day. Well done...Well done." Archie muttered as he gently guided the remaining herd through the large gate.

Gavin hefted the very tired and very relaxed Rebecca through her front door and sat her in a chair so he could remove her muddy shoes. She was still out cold, and Gavin noticed that half of her bright pink sweat suit was covered with a layer of thick mud from her brief nap on the road, so he gently removed most of her clothing. He was shocked to see the vast number of red, swollen bee stings covering her body.

He carried her to her bed, applied more of the pink lotion to the stings, and after it dried he covered her with the blankets. As a final gesture, he brushed that rebellious lock of auburn hair from her face before he turned to leave.

He wasn't prepared for her sudden, strong grip at the collar of his shirt pulling him toward her. "You...are a really sexy man." She slurred, as she smiled drunkenly into his beautiful face.

Gavin laughed and tried to pry her strong little fingers from his shirt. "Well, thank you."

Rebecca pulled him closer in an awkward attempt to kiss him.

Gavin released her death-grip and tucked her hands under the warmth of her blankets. "Darlin', as flattered as I am...you're three sheets to the wind. I prefer my women sober."

Her glazed-over eyes didn't seem to comprehend but with an "Ok", she closed them and snuggled into her covers.

As much as he wanted to kiss her, he was a gentleman, so he took the high road and left her alone. Gavin tossed her dirty clothes in the washing machine and scoped out the place for some food since he'd not eaten the entire day. He availed himself of some of the bread, butter and tea the landlord left Rebecca as a welcome gift.

In no time at all, the buzzer on the dryer called him to attention. Gavin folded her clothes and set them on a table in her room, covered her exposed shoulders with a blanket and watched her sleep for a moment. He shook his head at the strange affection he was beginning to feel for this woman.

Gavin wasn't delusional. He knew that he had just met her but he was very serious about getting to know her better. It wasn't that he was afraid to be in a relationship again; he just didn't want to play games anymore. He wanted to settle down, for good- in Scotland, and truth be told, he hadn't found anyone he was entirely interested in- until now. He gave her a chaste kiss on the forehead and placed a note on the pile of clothes with a mischievous grin before quietly closing the door behind him.

Chapter 8

The early morning sun poured through the bedroom window and I woke tired and disoriented. My mouth was dry and the room felt like it was spinning. I blinked my unfocused eyes and tried to get my foggy brain to register where I was. It wasn't until I caught a glimpse of a Highland cow chewing its cud right outside my window that I remembered.

With the realization that I was in Scotland, a flood of additional questions poured through my mind. First and foremost was, how the heck did I get into bed? I remembered the bees…And, I remembered Gavin and his motorcycle and his amazing eyes and sexy voice that sent electricity coursing through my body, but that was about it.

"Please let me be clothed," I whispered earnestly before lifting the sheets. I was…sort of. I had my cami and underwear on, but where did my other clothes go? I remember buying that horrible pink outfit but couldn't remember how I got out of it…

After staring out the window for a few more minutes, I decided to take a look around. I had no idea if I was in the cottage I had rented or not but I did remember the photos from the website and it looked vaguely similar. I stood and wrapped the quilted bedspread around me and wandered around the cozy bedroom.

The head of the wrought iron bed pressed up against a slanted ceiling leaving just enough room at the foot of the bed for a heavy wood armoire. The photos they posted online made the room look a lot bigger. There was one nightstand, which was large enough to hold a lamp and an alarm clock. On it, I saw a folded pile of clean clothes. There was a note on top.

Thank you for last night.
-Gavin

"Crap." I gathered my blanket tighter around myself. I couldn't have been that easy, I thought, but again, I couldn't remember a damn thing. Early onset Alzheimer's was on the top of my list of excuses, but clearly, I couldn't hold my liquor either…or antihistamine. I cringed to think of what else could've happened. Not that it would've been such a bad thing to have sex with Gavin. He was gorgeous. He was funny. He was perfect, really. I just wished that I could remember it.

I tossed the comforter on the bed and padded across the cold hardwood floor to the tiny bathroom and wedged myself between the toilet, sink and bathtub in order to shut the door. This was the smallest bathroom I had ever seen in my entire life.

When I turned to look in the mirror, I had forgotten that I had covered my face with Calamine lotion and, momentarily stunned, I screamed as I stumbled backward and nearly fell into the odd-sized bathtub. They must've built the bathroom around the thing. I grabbed at anything that would prevent me from falling all the way into the tub–which I did avoid– but I knocked the towel rack off of the wall and stubbed my toe on the toilet in the process. I let out a second scream of pain and moments later, the door burst open, knocking me fully into the bathtub.

It was Gavin wielding a not-so-dangerous looking butter knife.

"What's going on?"

"What the hell, Gavin?"

Gavin caught me sprawled *rather unsexily* in the bathtub and dropped the knife. "I heard screaming. You alright? "

"I was until you nearly killed me."

"You were makin' quite a racket in here." He offered his hand, and I took it.

He pulled me out of the tub into his arms. He smelled so good. Like leather and gasoline and rain. Now that I say that out loud it sounds kind of disgusting but it wasn't. It was amazing. I inhaled his scent and snuggled into his warmth. I wanted to kiss him—hell, I wanted to do much more than that to him—but. I didn't even know his last name. When I came to my senses I took a step back. Well, as far back as I could in the tiny bathroom. "Why are you still here?"

He smiled down at me. "I brought you a few groceries." His eyes drank their fill of my near nakedness. "You have a serious aversion to being clothed."

I shoved his very firm body out of the bathroom. "No. But for some reason every time you show up, my clothes have a way of being conveniently absent."

He waggled his eyebrows as he (not so discreetly) took in the view. "Aye. It's most certainly, very convenient."

I shut the door with more force than I probably needed to. "I need to take a shower…alone.'

"If you must."

*   *   *

Gavin convinced himself that he should keep the key to her house overnight *just in case* so he could check on her and make sure she was still alive in the morning. To his pleasant surprise, he found her very much alive.

Buying her groceries was an afterthought and after their very close encounter in the bathroom, he was very glad he had an excuse to stay a bit longer. He couldn't remember the last time he was so happy to be around someone. He didn't remember being this way with Emma, ever.

He was almost finished putting the groceries away when Rebecca found him in the kitchen. Her pink sweat suit definitely clung to her in all the right places. "You look amazing."

She smacked him on the chest playfully. "Did you lose your glasses?"

"I don't wear glasses."

"Well, you should start because I look hideous." Gavin walked toward her and she stepped around him. She opened the fridge in what appeared to be a subtle effort to place a barrier between them. "Thank you so much for the groceries."

"Aye." He moved toward Rebecca with the sexiest half-smirk across his face. His eyes full of the fire of life.

She laughed as her stomach rumbled. "I'm starving."

"I thought you might be."

Without taking his eyes off of her, Gavin dropped two thick slices of bread into the toaster. He already had a kettle of water boiling, which he poured over two tea bags.

Rebecca was really taken by how comfortable Gavin looked- in her kitchen- while he made breakfast for her. She couldn't remember the last time anyone took care of her just because. She knew she was walking into uncharted territory with him and she was very willing to move forward with him but she wanted to make sure that her choices were based in reality and that she wasn't projecting her version of a romantic fantasy on him. However, according to Gavin's note, it appeared they were now into the "let me make you breakfast" part of the relationship.

"How did I get here last night?"

"On the back of my motorcycle."

She accepted the cup of tea from Gavin's large, strong hands and sat at the table. "I remember that but…How did I get…into my house and into my bed and why were my clothes off? The last thing I remember were cows. Lots of cows."

Gavin's deep, rich laugh shook Rebecca. She loved his laugh. She wanted him to keep laughing.

He set the two pieces of perfectly toasted bread on a plate. "You were off your head."

"I was not."

"You were pissed." He sat across from her.

"I was medicated." Rebecca took a sip of tea.

"You think what you want Luv, if it'll make you feel better." He slathered one of the pieces of toast with butter and honey then handed it to Rebecca.

Under normal circumstances, Rebecca would have argued the point but she knew he was right. "I must have been *off my head* because I can't remember a thing." She took another sip of tea trying to act much cooler than she felt. "So, what did happen last night?"

Gavin looked over the edge of his cup playfully. "You remember nothing?"

"Nothing."

"Well then…" Gavin let his eyes wander over her body for a moment. "…I should probably tell you that…" He picked up his phone. "Oh, hold on."

It took her a minute to realize that he was pretending to text someone and she yanked his phone out of his hand. "Tell me."

Gavin enjoyed her feistiness. "Are you sure you want to know?"

"No. But tell me anyway."

He held her eyes for what seemed like an eternity then broke into a smile. "Nothing happened, Luv." She didn't look like she was buying it. "You tried to kiss me, but being the gentleman that I am, I fought you off."

Rebecca's body relaxed- a little. "I'm not sure if I should be embarrassed or relieved."

Gavin held out his hand for his phone. "A little of both, I'd wager. Do you have a boyfriend?"

"Nice non sequitur."

"Answer the question, please."

Rebecca relinquished the phone reluctantly then took a bite of the bread. "Mmmm. This is really good!"

"Boyfriend?"

Obviously, he wasn't going to relent. "Not anymore." She shrugged. "He sent me a rabbit."

Gavin wasn't following. "What did a rabbit have to do with it?"

"He broke up with me by attaching a note to a cute little rabbit."

"Really?"

"Yeah. True story."

"Is that an American thing?"

"No."

"Well, he sounds like a wanker."

Rebecca nodded her head and took a bite of the toast.

Gavin smiled his adorable half-smile and touched her hand. "I'm sorry…and incredibly pleased."

He was startled at how relieved he was that she didn't have a boyfriend. He was definitely drawn to this woman. It wasn't just her physical appearance it was her spirit; her laughter in the face of adversity that he was attracted to. The antihistamine had done its job and the swelling had gone down significantly. Her face looked much better than it did the day before, and he knew she was a beauty under all of the swelling. He didn't want to scare Rebecca away by being too forward too quickly and he withdrew his hand. "So, you came to Scotland to get away from it all then? Make a new start?"

"Not entirely. I came here to meet my father for the first time." She missed the warmth and pressure of his hand resting on hers.

"Took you a while, did it?

"I just found out a few days ago."

"Damn."

"Yeah. When I was a kid, my mother, in her infinite wisdom, told me I came from a sperm bank."

"Tidy." Was all he could think to say. "So, did you? Meet him yet?"

"Well, I've pretty much been with you since I arrived so I haven't had a lot of time." She flashed a smile and his heart leapt. "Besides, I wanted to get rid of this," she gestured to her swollen face, "before I met him for the first time."

Gavin nodded thoughtfully. "That's probably a good idea. I didn't know what to think when I first saw ya. Is it human.? Is it…?"

"Wanker."

"Quite possibly." Gavin stood and grabbed the kettle to pour more water in his cup. "There's an old Scottish sayin' that I think fits rather nicely in this situation. Bainne nan gobhar fo chobhar 's e blàth, 's e chuireadh an spionnadh sna daoine a bah."

Rebecca raised her eyebrows in confusion but kept silent.

"Aren't you going to ask me what it means?"

"Nope."

This woman was a cracker. He stared at her for a moment and nodded seriously. "Well, I'll tell you even though you don't deserve to know." He waited for a response…He received a nearly indistinguishable raise of a single eyebrow.

"It is the milk of the goat foamin' and warm, that gave the strength to the past generations of people..."

Rebecca gave him a blank stare. "That literally means nothing. There is no application there to anything we were just talking about."

"Aye, I know. I just wanted to wow you with a wee bit of Gaelic." He smirked. "Did I?"

"Absolutely." She said sarcastically. "I am completely undone." Rebecca giggled and popped the last bit of toast into her mouth. "This honey is amazing."

"Thank you. It's mine."

Rebecca licked the last bit of stickiness off of her fingers. "You're a beekeeper?"

"Aye. Among other things. An Effen beekeeper." He let out a light chortle.

"If you don't like being a beekeeper, why do you do it?"

"Not F-ing beekeeper Effen beekeeper."

"OK...And?"

Gavin smirked and cleared his throat. "He kept bees in the Scot's town of Effen. A wise *Effen beekeeper* was he. But one day this *Effen beekeeper, g*ot stung by a big Effen bee!"

"Oh, you were being funny."

She laughed and Gavin wished he could snap a photo of her without having it come off as creepy.

"You said you did other things in addition to being an *Effen beekeeper*. Other things like what?"

"It'll be easier to show ya. Fancy another ride on the motorcycle?"

Truth be told, she could hardly wait to have her arms wrapped around Gavin again, but she tried to respond with a neutral tone..."Sure."

Gavin held open the front door. "After you."

Rebecca knew she should slow things down with him. And she should probably spend some time thinking about meeting her father at some point since it was the reason she was in Scotland in the first place. But she decided that she would start that endeavor tomorrow. She climbed onto the motorcycle and leaned heavily against Gavin's back. She'd known him a day and already it felt so natural to be with him. She decided that she would take the "wee bit of advice" she had gotten from Niles, her friend on the airplane, and be a doer…not a thinker. It was time that she plunged into life, and relinquished her control to fate…or whatever.

Gavin patted her hands and took off. He found himself hopeful for the future for the first time in a long while.

Chapter 9

The castle ruins that came into view before Rebecca were the most beautiful sight she had ever seen. The ruins perched perilously close to the edge a cliff, daring a stiff wind to topple them over into the tumultuous sea below. The light stone reflected the gold of the sun and the green hills were lush and welcoming. The light that touched the tops of the hills left the valley in shadows. As they got closer to the ruins, Rebecca could see several smaller outbuildings and the remains of a barn. Her writer's mind was going a hundred miles an hour.

Gavin stopped the motorcycle in the dirt parking lot and pointed up a very long, very steep pathway climbing up to the castle. "Want to give it a go?"

Her eyes were on fire with excitement. "Absolutely. The view must be amazing!" Rebecca took off up the hill and Gavin followed- very much enjoying his view.

"Aye. It certainly is." He smirked and continued after her.

When Rebecca reached the top she took in the 360-degree view. She could see for miles in every direction. She breathed in the moist, salty sea air. "I was right. This is absolutely amazing!"

Gavin was struck by the intense blue of her eyes as they caressed the landscape. He felt so comfortable around her. So familiar, like he had known her forever.

"Thank you so much for this. It's breathtaking." The sky looked like rain and the wind was picking up, but that didn't seem to bother her as she snapped a few photos.

Gavin watched her small fingers brush the wind-swept hair from her face. He pulled out his phone and snapped a photo of her. "It's hard to match something that beautiful in a photo."

Rebecca nodded. "Exactly what I was just thinking!" She stared at him for a moment and noticed that he was not talking about her photos.

"So what do you do, Becca? Other than playing the damsel in distress, of course?"

"I'm a writer. Well, I was…Actually, I guess I'm trying to be one again. I gave it a break for a couple of years but now I have this story in my head and I can't stop thinking about it." She looked out toward the darkening sea. "This is where my love story begins." She smiled sweetly up at him.

Gavin choked a bit. Did he hear her right? Could she possibly be feeling the same way about him? "Love story?"

"Yeah. It's a medieval romance of sorts…Dragons, knights. You know. I'm so glad I decided to come to Scotland. I never could've described this beauty adequately from photos."

"Ah…right…right." Gavin looked over the grand expanse, wishing that she'd been talking about him. "I like to imagine what it must've been like for the generations of people who lived and loved and lost their lives here." He met Rebecca's eyes.

Rebecca couldn't look away. That was literally the exact same thing she was thinking yesterday on the back of his motorcycle. They were already sharing a brain. She felt like she was teetering on the proverbial diving board ready to jump, head-first, into the unknown with Gavin. Rebecca stared into the depths of his beautiful green eyes and was reticent to look away.

Gavin broke first to look at the rapidly darkening sky.

"So what else do you do besides rescuing damsels in distress? Oh, and keeping bees."

Gavin laughed. "I manage a bit of property. Also been trying my hand at truffle farming. You know, workin' the land."

"Quite a manly occupation."

"Aye." Gavin gestured toward the path. "Shall we walk?"

"Sure." Rebecca followed Gavin. "I'm just blown away to think that someone used to own all of this land."

Gavin smiled down at her. "Someone still does."

It took her a minute to register what he was saying. "You? No way." She took in the land with a different set of eyes. "This is not a 'bit' of property just FYI."

Gavin loved this land and would do anything to protect it but things were getting difficult to manage even with the profits from the small family-run apiary. "I'm afraid it's a bit of an albatross around our necks at the moment."

"But it's so amazing." She wanted to pitch a tent right where she stood and stay there forever. Well, maybe not today. The sea and sky were both looking bleak.

"Amazing yes, but I'd like to give this bit to the National Trust. If not, we may lose all of it."

"National Trust?"

"It's a conservation group dedicated to preserving the history of our nation by taking on the responsibility of upkeep on certain properties." Gavin leaned against the rock and took in the area around him with a look Rebecca couldn't quite place. Sadness? Irritation? Nostalgia?

"I think that's a great idea. Everyone should experience this place." Rebecca sat down on a large boulder overlooking the darkening sea below and took a deep breath. "It's absolutely incredible."

"I agree with you, but my father has other ideas and is digging his heels in."

"Like what?"

"Well, I think he's holding out hope that I stumble upon and somehow marry a rich American."

"How very Downton Abbey of you."

"Aye."

"I happen to be American." Did she just say that out loud?

"Aye?"

Rebecca didn't know how to respond but thankfully, didn't have time to worry overly long about it.

"Time to run." Gavin grabbed Rebecca's hand and pulled her toward a small nearby enclosure right before the clouds broke lose in sheets of rain. Rebecca watched Gavin's muscles ripple gently under his fitted sweatshirt as he brushed the cobwebs away from their entrance. How the hell would she say no to this guy if he tried to kiss her? The answer was: She wouldn't. She knew herself. She could text Lacy and ask her for her opinion on the matter, but she also knew what Lacy would say. She'd tell her to go for it.

Rebecca hugged her pink jacket around her and stood at the entrance of the enclosure, just out of the wind's reach, watching as the dark rain enveloped the beautiful emerald grass and golden castle.

Gavin watched her. The desire to wrap his arms around her was so strong. He couldn't take his eyes off of her. She was absolutely breathtaking. "The Scots have a saying, 'if ya don't like the weather now wait twenty minutes and it'll be different.'" He wasn't sure what possessed him to rattle off inane sayings around Rebecca.

Rebecca felt Gavin looking at her and she turned to see him smiling broadly down at her. She looked into his eyes and her heart stopped for a moment. A perfect moment.

An owl screeched past them as it exited the darkness behind Gavin. Its wingspan was massive. Rebecca jumped and reflexively, Gavin pulled her body protectively into his, turning his back on the creature.

Rebecca found herself pinned between the wall and Gavin's warm, muscular body. The uneven rocks of the wall were jabbing painfully into her back but she was afraid to move or breathe for fear that Gavin would let go. She saw her desire reflected back at her when they locked eyes.

Their closeness was electric. Gavin thought his heart was going to burst if he didn't kiss her. This connection between the two of them was too strong to resist any longer. *To hell with it,* he thought and bent to kiss her.

"You are so incredibly beautiful."

As she leaned in to close the distance between them a familiar *buzzing sound* hit Rebecca's ear.

"Bees!" She propelled Gavin away from her so furiously she almost knocked him into the cave wall on the other side. She was strong. She ran out of the cave flailing her arms— screaming and stripping her clothing off.

Gavin stood for a moment and waved a single bee away from his face as he watched this *lass wi a heed full 'o bees* stripping down to her knickers…again. "This is becoming a habit," he yelled after her and resumed his previous duty of picking up her discarded clothing. "I quite like it."

Following her trajectory, he assumed Rebecca would be back at the motorcycle so he wasn't surprised when he found her there- half naked and cold and shivering.

Rebecca smiled and shrugged. Damn, she was irresistible.

After Rebecca had re-clothed herself, Gavin removed his leather jacket from the saddle bag and zipped it around her. He still wanted to kiss her, but her lips were turning blue with cold, and instead, he hurried to start the motorcycle.

It was a cold, rainy ride back to Rebecca's. Gavin was hoping he could get another week of good weather to ride his motorcycle this year, but he knew that today was probably his last day on it. The weather was getting more and more unpredictable. Ned, the pub owner/mechanic/lawyer had assured him that the weather would hold for another few days and that there would be very little rain. Ned was also a bit of a weatherman of sorts in addition to fixing cars and lawyering, but Ned was clearly wrong this time.

"You wanna come in?" She bit her blue lip in an attempt to appear nonchalant about the invitation, which only made her even more alluring to Gavin. He nodded, pushed through the door and his hands instantly found a home around her waist. He pulled her tightly against him and kissed her with an intensity that shocked them both.

His lips were amazing. They were as soft as she thought they'd be, and she was getting lost in a sensation that she never remembered having before. It was the kind of kiss she'd always hoped for but could have never imagined. There was a spark between them and she knew he felt it, too.

Gavin trailed his lips down her neck and he caressed her back and neck tenderly with his large hands, warming her inside and out.

They were both soaked to the bone so it was only natural that they strip the offending articles of clothing off of each other. Other than her tank and underwear, Rebecca couldn't seem to stay clothed around this guy.

She'd bet her life he had one hell of a six pack.

Rebecca slid her hands up his chest and removed his t-shirt. Yep. One hell of a six-pack. Feeling his warmth, she remembered the first time she hugged him. She trailed her lips softly across his chest savoring his scent. He let out a deep groan and claimed her mouth with new intensity.

She was shocked at how right he felt but she needed to stop and if she didn't stop things now, she wouldn't be able to stop at all.

She removed her hands, that had, without her knowledge, made their way to the waistband of his nicely-fitted jeans and gently pressed them against his beautifully firm chest and pushed him away, very reluctantly.

"We need to talk first." She could barely speak, he had her quite out of breath.

"Why? You a virgin?" He smirked- sufficiently out of breath as well.

She laughed. "No. But I'm American…you're Scottish."

"Master of the bleedin' obvious you are." He laughed heartily and moved in to kiss her again.

"Let me finish." She touched his lips with her finger, which he promptly kissed.

He locked her eyes with a glint, obviously not listening to a word she was saying then trailed kisses down her neck. "Aye. Finish."

…Which had the appropriate effect of making Rebecca question why she wanted to stop this bliss in the first place. She took a fortifying breath and stepped back, just out of his reach.

He caressed her with his eyes, which were just as dangerous as those lips of his. "God, you're beautiful."

He was next to her quicker than she had a chance to think so she blurted out the only thing on her mind at the moment. "Do you have protection with you?"

Gavin shook his head. "No." He wished he'd had the aforethought to purchase a box of condoms since he'd met Rebecca. He'd had several opportunities.

"I don't have any either." She stepped around him and looked around for something to distract them. "Tea?"

Gavin nodded in resignation.

She poured water over two teabags. "I really like you and I want to get to know you better before we..." She looked toward the bedroom for emphasis.

Gavin threw her his amazing half smile. "What makes you think I'm that type of man?"

"Well, I just kissed you and anyone who kisses like that..." She shrugged and set the two cups on the table.

"I want to get to know you as well." Gavin leaned in and kissed her again. But this time it was gentle, soft.

She gave into the sensation and when he pulled away to look into her eyes she actually stopped breathing for a minute. No one had ever looked at her like that.

"You are so beautiful."

Trying to save what was left of her resolve, she smirked. "We've already established that you need glasses."

Gavin took a deep breath and cupped her face in his hands. "As luck would have it, I will be out of town for a couple of days." He pressed a kiss to her forehead, took a sip of tea and picked up his clothes from the floor. Rebecca wasn't excessively happy that he was getting dressed. "But when I return, I most definitely want to pick this up, most preferably where we left off."

Rebecca walked him to the door. "I was thinking the same thing."

Rebecca watched Gavin leave from her front steps and laughed out loud with the realization that she could blame this entire trip on her inability to hold her liquor...or antihistamines. This trip had been one disaster after another, and there was no way she could have even come close to writing something like this. But as physically painful and uncomfortable as her circumstances had been, she wouldn't change a thing.

She wanted to see where things would go with Gavin. He was definitely a man among men.

She smiled in thankfulness at the quaint neighborhood that she would call home for a while and her eye caught some movement from one of the windows across the street. Seeing a curious neighbor, Rebecca waved. The curtains swished abruptly shut.

* * *

Evelyn, the neighbor across the street, peered at Rebecca suspiciously from behind her curtains. She heard from the neighbors that a foreigner would be living there for several months while they were out of the country. They said she would be working from her house. What the woman did for work, Evelyn could only guess after seeing Gavin exit in an uncharacteristically disheveled state. Evelyn thought the woman must have seen her because she was waving in her direction. She quickly swished the curtains shut.

"Archie," Evelyn bellowed heartily at her husband. "Archie!"

Archie shuffled his thin wrinkled frame toward his cacophonous wife of fifty years. "I'm here, you don't need to yell."

"Took ya bloody well long enough." She pointed through a slit in the curtains. "The foreigner has arrived."

Archie nodded in understanding but wasn't quite sure why this revelation was so important as to have pulled him away from watching reruns of his favorite TV show, *Ballykissangel*. "Why'd ya get me off my chair woman? You couldn't've brought this life altering news to me your wee little self?" He kissed his woman on the forehead.

"Aye, but I wanted ye to see her for yourself so you kenned who to watch when the time came."

Archie smiled at Evelyn's taste for the sinister. "Aye, I met the lass yesterday. A wee bit of a drinking problem from the looks of it."

"She's gotta be Irish." Evelyn nodded with assurance not taking her eyes off of the cottage. "Well, we don't want any of that here now, do we?"

Archie shook his head and walked toward the television. "Come to the TV room now luv. We'll watch your favorite Broadchurch episodes today."

With one final glance at Rebecca's now empty front stoop, Evelyn followed her man into the next room.

Chapter 10

The incessant ringing of the home phone jolted me out of my exhaustion coma the next morning. I pulled back the covers, then immediately changed my mind and dug myself further into the warmth of the bed, but the phone would not stop. I looked at the windup clock on my dresser–it read seven o'clock in the morning.

I climbed out of bed and unpleasantly placed my bare feet on the cold, wooden floor and padded quickly to the phone. "Hello?"

The voice on the other end was low and jolly. "Is this Rebecca?"

"Yes," I said warily. I was more than a little confused. "How did you get this number?" I picked up the ancient black rotary phone and turned it over in my hand looking for a number. "I don't even know this number." I set the phone down and realized the man on the other end called me by my first name. Creepy. "Wait. How do you know my name?"

He laughed heartily. "'Tis a small town, luv. We know everyone here at the pub."

"The pub? Oh! The Fox and Hen." The light went on. "You have my car."

"Aye. That I do. And it's ready. Name's Ned, by the way. You were lucky, only a few scratches on the front. Just finished vacuuming out the bees- poor things. You need to come get it now. Don't have the room to store it for long."

"Oh. Okay. Great. Where are you exactly?"

"We're near the Glen Hotel, on the main street."

I had no idea where I was, nor did I have any idea where this supposed town landmark was either. "How far is that from where I'm staying?"

"Hell if I know, woman." Ned didn't bother to cover the phone before he yelled to whom I could only suppose were the early morning patrons of his pub. "Any of you know how far the McGerry cottage is?"

I could barely hear the reply in the background. "Aye, it's about four miles to the south of us."

Ned got back on the phone. "Four miles, south."

I nodded at the information. Four miles would be an easy walk. "Thank you. I'll be there later today."

He took a deep breath. "You know your suitcase is too big for that car."

I wasn't totally sure how I should respond, so I pretended not to hear him and hung up the phone. I got dressed and mapped the directions for the Fox and Hen on my phone. Walking four miles shouldn't take me too long.

Two hours later, I was seriously reconsidering my wisdom in walking four miles. The only shoes I had were the pair of slip-ons I wore when I traveled so I could be more efficient in the airport screening lines, and I was starting to get blisters. The other little issue at hand was that I had no idea where I was...I was totally lost. My phone died an hour into the walk and I hadn't seen a single car or another house since I left my neighborhood.

I sat on a boulder and slipped off my shoe. There was a large blister forming on my heel, and I knew I couldn't continue much longer on it. I decided barefoot was probably the best option to save myself the future pain.

Several hours later...the sun was beginning to descend and it was starting to get cold. If that weren't bad enough, the rocky surface was doing a number on the soles of my feet so I had another go with the shoes. I shoved a leaf between my blister and my shoe and it seemed to be working, but I was starting to get a bit panicked. I didn't know where I was, had no cell service, no map and I was super thirsty. Thankfully, it wasn't raining.

The sound of a man's voice behind me startled me. "You lost, Pet?"

I turned to see a gorgeously cut Scotsman with a mischievous smile leaning out of the window of a white cargo van. These handsome Scotsmen and their mischievous smiles. What was up with that?

"No, just sightseeing." I was so relieved to see another human I would have hugged him if he had been standing near me.

"Have you seen enough?"

I nodded and tried to compose myself so I could assess my current predicament: Empty street, single woman, single man, white cargo van with no windows in the back... Ideal situation. What was it with this country? Were there no women anywhere?

"What are you doing way out here anyway?"

I shrugged. "I'm walking to Newtonmore."

He laughed. "No Pet, you're walkin' further into Cairngorm." He pointed behind him. "Newtonmore is the other direction."

I was less than enthused. "You've got to be kidding me."

"No. Not at all."

"I'm heading into Newtonmore. You can ride with me."

I looked toward the back of the *kidnapper van* and shook my head slowly. "Thank you, but I'll be fine."

"Suit yourself, but there's rarely a soul on this road."

I knew that to be a very true statement. There was no-one around. That was the issue. No-one would see me get into this guy's car. No-one would know to look for me out here. My phone was dead so I couldn't even text Lacy a photo of the guy's face with a text that would read: *If you don't hear from me in 3 hours this is the guy who killed me.*

Necessity gave way to reason and I reluctantly agreed to his help. I had already made a series of poor choices since I decided to head to Scotland, and I prayed that this decision wouldn't be my last.

I opened the passenger door. I paused again before climbing in and looked up and down the road. Not a soul. I sighed and climbed in.

"I'm Patrick."

"Rebecca."

He pointed to my seatbelt. "Hook in."

Right before we took off, another car passed us heading the same direction. It was that older couple who lived across the street from my house. What were the odds? I rolled the window down and almost fell out of it as I waved to them hoping they would stop so I could catch a ride with them. The woman just glared at me and said something to the old man who was driving. I wished I had caught their names so I could yell after them to wait.

I stared at Patrick while I fished through my purse for my keys; which I threaded between my fingers like the Wolverine from X-Men. "Just so you know…there are now two witnesses who have seen me with you. In fact, I think they live across the street from me."

Patrick shot me an unsettling look. "Oh, you mean Evelyn and Archie? Cute couple. Thank you for pointing them out." He noticed the precautionary key *weapon* in my hand. "I'll have to kill them, too."

He laughed like a baddie and I tightened my grip on the keys as I tried to unlock the door. "Stay away from me!"

Patrick grabbed my wrist and burst out laughing. "Relax, Pet. I was only takin' a piss."

I looked into his eyes to discern his earnestness and removed my wrist from his grip. "Not funny."

He laughed and smiled unaffectedly.

When we walked through the door of the Fox and Hen, I felt like I had entered another realm. The floor was covered with dark, grooved planks that looked to be hundreds of years old, and the ceilings were supported by large wooden beams. The bench seats were showing centuries of wear. The small low-ceilinged pub was filled to the brim with young and old alike, all yelling at the smallish television situated above the long rough-hewn bar. A football game was in full swing and the loyalties of each fan were evident in the respective Hibernian and Celtics jerseys each patron was sporting. The young men at the bar were particularly loud especially after the Celtics scored.

An older man standing behind the bar, dressed in greasy overalls and a tie, yelled at the loudest young man in the group. "Ewan, shut yer trap and help out your sister!" He pointed to a beautiful redhead who was carrying an overloaded tray filled with a massive number of drinks through the crowd.

Ewan downed the rest of his pint. "Aye. I'm just finishin' my break." Ewan stood and patted his pal on the back- who happened to be wearing a Hibernian jersey. "That'll be twenty quid for the game."

His friend shook his head. "Ya still owe me a packet from the last game, ya tosser."

"Aye. And you owe me from the game before." His friend nodded and that was the end of that. I caught myself smiling at the ease with which the matter was settled.

Patrick caught Ned's eye and nodded. "Ned is just there. Tie and overalls." Patrick said, like it was no big thing to wear overalls with a tie.

Ned nodded back at Patrick and walked toward the two of us.

"Rebecca, I assume?" Ned held out his hand palm up.

I took his hand and shook it. "Yes. Nice to meet you."

"Your car's 'round back." He retrieved his hand and placed it in front of me - again palm up. "But first, let's settle the matter of the hundred pounds you owe me for the tow and the check-up."

I felt stupid for not reading him better and pulled a one-hundred-pound note out of my purse. "Oh, yes. Of course."

Without ceremony, Ned pocketed the money and addressed Patrick before heading toward the bar. "Were you able to acquire the items we talked about?"

The glint in his eye said much in terms of secrecy. "Aye."

Ned was similarly discreet and looked around cautiously. They were obviously up to something. "Bring 'em round back."

"Aye. Straight away."

A haggard middle-aged woman sitting at the end of the bar nearly fell off backward swigging on her pint, but Ewan, carrying a tray of drinks, caught her with his free hand mid-fall as he passed by and steadied her on the stool before continuing on. "Fit like, Maggie?"

"Ach. Away ye go!"

Ewan was unfazed and continued on his rounds, chatting jovially with the patrons.

With a hand on the small of my back, Patrick guided me toward the bar.

The beautiful redhead tending bar, glared daggers at him and filled up a pint without looking at it. "Draft?" she asked rhetorically as she slammed the drink down on the bar in front of him, spilling off some of the foam.

Patrick backed away before he could get splashed. "Easy now, Kara."

Without hearing him, she turned her attention to me. "You look like you could use a stiff one."

Patrick took that opportunity to wink suggestively at me. Kara was fuming. It was clear that there had been something between the two of them. And it was clear that it was over—at least for Patrick.

Patrick seemed a bit rough around the edges, but there was an ease about him that I found intriguing. There was a lot more about the man that I found unsettling. He leaned into my ear, "I'll be just a minute." And he left the bar.

Kara coughed her impatience. "To drink? What do you want?"

"Oh. Sorry. Just an orange juice. Do you have organic orange juice, by chance?…No pulp?"

Kara stared at me as if I had ordered in a foreign language. Without saying a word, she reached under the counter and plopped a whole orange on the bar in front of me with an *I dare you to complain* look. Her eyes locked with mine.

I took a deep breath and didn't look away. "Do you have a straw?"

Kara let out a hearty laugh and immediately softened. "What the hell happened to your face?"

These Scots were masters of the non sequitur. "I crashed into a crap-ton of bees."

"Well, you look terrible."

And they were incredibly subtle people as well.

I laughed. "You should see the bees."

This last statement was punctuated by a loud burp emanating from deep within the belly of dear, disheveled Maggie.

"Dammit Maggie. Put that drink down. I don't wanna have to cover your shift at the hospital again."

Maggie took the last swig of her beer and wiped her face with the sleeve of her nurse's scrubs. "Don't get your knickers in a twist. Been at that hospital thirty years and never killed anyone."

"Yet." Ewan quipped as he passed.

Maggie may have been sloshed, but that didn't stop her from connecting her hand to the back of Ewan's head in a playful smack.

I peeled my orange and shrugged at Kara. "You also work at a hospital?"

Kara nodded. "I'm a nurse. So is Maggie. I help my dad, Ned, here at the pub to subsidize the income…NHS. Ya know?"

Maggie stood on wobbly legs and shuffled toward the front door.

Kara watched Maggie repeatedly push the door. Ewan yelled from across the room. "Pull, Maggie." And she pulled the door, stumbling onto the sidewalk.

"I'm gonna have to go in. She's gonna end up in a ditch, two blocks from the hospital…again."

Patrick slapped some money on the counter in front of Kara and pointed with amusement to the pile of orange peel in front of me, indicating that he was picking up my tab as well. His phone rang and he looked with apprehension at the caller ID. "Damn awful reception in here. I need to rush off." He locked eyes with me. "I'll see you later, yeah?" I nodded and Patrick kissed me on the cheek. He threw his final comment to Kara as he parted. "Tell Ned I'll bring the rest tomorrow."

Kara scowled after him and then turned toward me with a concerned look. "You should watch out for that one. He's a wide boy."

I nodded absently as I watched the fine figure depart. "He's a what?"

"Wide boy." Giving no further explanation, Kara turned and exited into the room behind the bar at the same time Ned walked through the front door and handed me my keys. "Car's out front. Convertible's a total waste of money here in Scotland, if ya ask me."

Kara reappeared with a purse slung over her shoulder and shot a look at Ned. "Well, she didn't ask ya now, did she, Dad?"

He jerked his head in the direction of my convertible. "Do 'ye not know that Scotland is one of the rainiest places on the earth? The Highlands being the worst."

"I didn't really think about it." I didn't remember buying it in the first place, but I wasn't about to admit that to anyone, anytime soon.

He shook his head and looked into the sky. "Ye best be putting that top up. We'll be havin' a wee bit of rain later. All week more like."

I looked out the window at the bright blue sky and nodded suspiciously. There wasn't a cloud to be seen. "Okay."

"I feel it in my bad knee. Never been wrong."

"That's because it's always raining in Scotland." Kara tossed the comment to Ned before nodding toward my car. "I need a ride to the hospital. I know Maggie isn't gonna make it." She yelled across the bar to Ewan. "Ewan, you'll lock up tonight. I'm leavin'."

"Ah, Kara. I've got a date with Suzie tonight."

"Well, ya don't anymore." And with that, Kara nudged me out of the pub. She held out her hand. "I'll be drivin'." Which left me in the passenger seat with a giant suitcase on my lap.

After I left Kara at the hospital, I drove around town trying to get my bearings. Newtonmore was a quaint town with one main road that I decided to call Main Street because I couldn't find a street sign. It housed a bakery, post office, hotel, restaurant and museum. The pub was on the opposite side of town from the hospital, and the cottage I was renting was further out of town apparently closer to Kingussie- toward the national forest.

The temperature was dropping and the air was moist but the scenery was amazing and I caught myself zoning out again as I watched the sun set in front of me. I managed to find my way home without too many missed turns and pulled into my driveway at last- just as it began to downpour. The rain hit me hard and fast and soaked me before I could park the car. After wrestling with my enormous passenger-side suitcase and taking way to many trips from my car to the front porch, I finally got everything inside and shut the door behind me. I caught my breath as I drenched the floor in the quaint living room.

Chapter 11

I was alone in Scotland and I loved it. I started a fire, boiled a kettle of water, fixed more toast with honey and made myself a cup of Nescafe. It sort of tasted like coffee. I'd always preferred coffee to tea, but after drinking this stuff, I poured it out and made a cup of tea. I gripped my cup to my chest and soaked in the warmth. I fully understood the reason everyone drank so much tea all of the time. It's because it was so damn cold and rainy here.

This wasn't the warm rain we had in Santa Barbara. This was a thick, chilled rain. Like laying in a bathtub of cold, split-pea soup. To be honest, I didn't recall being truly warm in the past several days. I re-stoked the fire, snuggled into a down blanket and pulled out my computer to write. I knew why so many of the great writers (J.M Barrie, Robert Louis Stevenson and Arthur Conan Doyle to name a few) were from this country: It was too *bloody* cold and wet to be anywhere else but in front of a fireplace drinking tea.

The flicker of the fire was mesmerizing and I began thinking of Abigail and the new character I was introducing: Ciro the dragon.

On a particularly stormy day, Abigail was hiding in the tower, trying to avoid the same conversation with her father that they had every day.

"You must marry."

"I will only marry if I fall in love."

"That is most unreasonable." And on and on it went...

As she began pacing at the top of the keep, she heard a horrific noise. She turned her head toward the screech to see what it was and was snatched into the talons of a horrible beast. A dragon. With eyes as blue as the sea and scales that shown like the sun. If she weren't so terrified she would have thought the dragon beautiful. But she was terrified. Abigail screamed and the dragon spoke. "You must be quiet, lady Abigail. You do not want Balthazar to hear you."

His voice was soothing and peaceful and had the most unique timbre. It sounded so rich and full of love that Abigail was no longer frightened of it. She knew she must have been imagining things because first of all, dragons didn't speak and second, it was a horrific beast who was speaking. "Who is Balthazar?"

"He is the evil wizard who put a spell on me five-hundred years ago that turned me into the creature you see before you."

Abigail accepted his answer and complied obediently to be silent for the rest of the journey, and before long she had been taken to a dark cave hidden deep inside the base of the hill. She thought this was an odd place for a dragon to live.

Before Abigail could fully process what was happening she was inside the dragon's lair: A dark cave hidden deep within the base of a mountain.

"My name," he told her, "is Ciro. I mean you no harm." He divulged to her that he rescued her from certain death. An army of Vikings was approaching from the north and they were just days away from sacking the castle.

Ciro had been watching the sweet Abigail for years now. He had fallen deeply in love with her but did not want to tell her for fear of losing her.

"What did you do to make the wizard angry enough to turn you into such a beast?"

"I was arrogant and prideful and my arrogance killed his beloved."

"So you are doomed to live like this forever?'

"No, it turns out that the wizard was a bit of a romantic and gave me a way out but only after I had mended my ways and became an honorable man...Well, dragon."

"What do you have to do?"

"I don't have to do anything. That's the difficult part."

"So what's to be done then?"

Ciro was mesmerized with the beauty of this glorious princess sitting before him. Her features were scrunched in determination while trying help him find a way out of his circumstance. "What can be done?"

"Nothing can be done."

"Nay, Ciro. You must have hope."

It has been five-hundred years. I see no hope."

She squared her shoulders. "Then you must tell me what someone else must do and I will do it for you."

"It's not as easy as that, dear, sweet Abigail. Though I do wish you could be the one to help."

"Then tell me and I will."

"Alas, I cannot divulge the secret to my release or all will be for naught."

She took a deep breath and sighed in resignation.

If only she would be the one to love him. To be the one to break the wizard's spell. He had to keep her hidden from Balthazar because, although Balthazar was a bit of a romantic, he was also heartbroken, vindictive and frankly, pure evil. Oh, and there was the bit about if the spell were broken over Ciro's life, it would consequently end the life of Balthazar.

* * *

I woke up in the middle of the night to a loud crash and flash of lightning. I found that I was still sitting in the chair in front of the waning fire. I grabbed the blanket tightly around me, added a few more logs to the fire and shuffled sleepily to the window where I could feel the vibrations of the rain pelting the cold, stiff window glass. It was hitting so hard that I thought the window might break.

There was no light in the cold darkness until another loud rumble vibrated through the house. The thunder was immediately followed by a static ripping sound right as a flash of extremely bright white light split the sky. The closeness of the lightning strike was a bit unnerving and I was now fully awake.

Since I could no longer sleep, I logged in to Skype. I looked at the clock; It was 7 pm in California. Lacy should be near her computer. I had so much to tell her. But what I really wanted to do was talk to Gavin. I wanted to hear his beautiful voice. It was three in the morning and I assumed he would be asleep, so instead, I decided to Skype Lacy. The *bloop* of the Skype connection was followed by a familiar "Hello girl," and the screen-sized face of a smiling Lacy appeared a second later.

"Hey, Lace."

Lacy's eyes grew wide. "Your face!?"

"I got stung."

"I'd say…" Lacy stared at me. "You look like a zit-faced adolescent."

"You're hilarious." I wasn't laughing.

"What time is it there?"

"Three a.m." I yawned and hugged my comforter tightly around me.

"Jet lag sucks."

"This time, it was the insane thunder that woke me up. It shook my whole house." I spun the computer around so Lacy could see my room.

"Super cute." She beamed through the computer screen. "So tell me about this hottie Scot you sent me the photo of! Damn, girl."

"Damn is right." Lacy gave me a knowing smile. "I know what you're thinking and it's still a bit early for all of that being in love stuff."

"Don't second-guess yourself Becks. You only have the one life to live, you know. Speaking of lives, have you met your dad yet?"

"No." I yawned. "I still look like I have a disease. You should've seen me yesterday. I'll get up there soon. I have a few months."

"Well, don't wait too long." Lacy picked up the laptop and moved to her couch.

"Hey! How's your new car? Have you been able to drive with your top down at all?"

"Yes. It is so beautiful here…I think I'm finally getting the…" I darted away from the computer. "OH CRAP!"

I was so tired from my *stroll* through the National Forest and the encounter with Patrick, and the cultural overload in the pub, and trying to get out of the deluge last night, that I forgot my car was still topless. Lacy jumped noticeably when my crazed expression showed back up on the screen. "I'll call you later." I slapped the lid of the computer shut, grabbed my car keys and launched myself toward the front door.

Apparently, the thunder must have woken up my neighbors, Archie and Evelyn as well. As I struggled with the top of my convertible in the inundation of Scottish rain, I saw him smile and nod as he watched me through the curtains. Evelyn shook her head as if to scold me for being an idiot and she walked away.

Chapter 12

Eating at the Fox and Hen the next day was a new experience. I pushed the black disk of whatever-the-heck-it-was around my plate. I figured that since I was in Scotland, I would embrace the culture with my entire being so, I ordered the full Scottish breakfast.

Kara set the bill on the table and I grabbed her sleeve before she was able to leave. "What is this?" I asked indicating the disc.

"Well, Luv, that's black pudding."

I liked pudding and was fairly certain that this was not pudding.

Seeing the question in my eyes she answered more fully. "It's made with pig's blood, suet and oatmeal."

I moved the plate to the center of the table. Kara laughed and indicated the bill. "Whenever you're ready."

I pulled out some bills and handed them to Kara. "Keep the change."

"Cheers. So what brings you to our wee town?"

"I came here to meet my father."

Unannounced and uninvited, Patrick slid into the bench across from me. "You're a Scottish lass?" He nodded to Kara. "A cup o' tea, pet. You know how I like it."

Kara narrowed her eyes at Patrick and mumbled, "Wanker" as she walked toward the bar.

I shook my head. "She's gonna spit in your tea."

"It's quite possible." Patrick slid my half-eaten breakfast toward himself and took a bite of the blood pudding without asking me for permission. Not that I had a problem with it, but it was really presumptuous of him. I nearly gagged.

"So, Scottish?'

"Yep. Apparently, I am of the Clan McDermott," I said the last bit with a terrible Scottish accent.

"Have you been to see him yet?"

"No, he doesn't know I'm here." My phone beeped with a text. It was a photo of Gavin smiling like the Cheshire Cat, holding a white rabbit. The accompanying text read, "Is this yours?" I laughed out loud.

"What's that?"

"It's my friend, Gavin." I held up the photo. "Do you know him?"

Patrick nodded and gave me a strange look before shoving the plate to the side. "Aye. We go back a long, long time."

"He's kinda awesome."

Patrick narrowed his eyes inquisitively. "How well do you know him?"

"Not very. He's really sweet, though."

"Sometimes things are not always as they seem." Patrick caught Kara's attention and indicated that he changed his mind on the tea. "I've got some deliveries to make today. Come with me." Patrick stood, and held his hand out to me very gallantly.

Since I had nothing else to do at the moment I figured I might as well take a drive around the area with someone who actually knew where he was going and to be honest, I was a bit terrified to drive at the moment. I shrugged. "Sure."

"Have you lived here your entire life?" We climbed into his van.

"Mostly."

It was strange getting only single word answers from him since he'd talked my ear off on the ride to the pub yesterday. I thought it was odd that he invited me to come with him since it really appeared that he didn't want the company.

Since we were effectively ignoring one another, I looked out the window wishing I could see more of the beautiful countryside, but all I could see were sheets of rain and a thick, gray mist coming up from the nearby river. It reminded me of the landscape near where I pictured Ciro dwelt and I couldn't help zoning out.

Weeks ran into months and Abigail was getting worried for her father. Ciro had told her of the siege and Abigail begged him to see how her castle faired. The news was not good. There was no castle left but there were rumors that the princess was dead and the king was alive in a neighboring kingdom.

"He must be distraught. I am all he had left after my mother died."

"I am afraid I do not know the answer to that question."

"I must leave and see for myself."

Ciro had grown to love Abigail more than life itself. He had never felt this way about anyone before. Not even his own wife. Of course, that was over 500 years ago, and she was long dead and it was an arranged marriage to the princess of another realm in an effort to proffer an alliance.

"Give me three days to think on how to proceed."

"I will. Thank you." Abigail kissed one of the scales on Ciro's face. She said that was her favorite scale because it had an odd freckle in the shape of a heart. She also liked to look into Ciro's blue eyes and note the interesting constellation-like dots. There wasn't much else to do but talk and count dots. And they did talk. They both shared their souls with each other without even realizing it.

Patrick's tire hit a rather large pothole and jarred me back to reality.

"Remind me to tell someone about that."

I nodded absently and continued looking out the window.

Throughout my *vast* history with men, I often found myself choosing the *bad-boy* type, and Patrick did seem to fit that description. I Googled the term *wide-boy* the second I got back to my cottage the day before and found it meant a *wheeler-dealer*. I was surprised to note that I wasn't remotely interested in Patrick. Yes, he was a specimen, and seemingly my type, but from the moment I met Gavin, I was only interested in him.

Although I didn't know anything about Gavin, I could really see myself dating him eventually. He was down to earth, funny and he was my first experience with an actual knight-in-shining-armor-on-a-white-horse type of guy. I guess leather and a motorcycle would probably be more accurate, but whatever. Gavin was real, and I felt there was something real between us. As much as I wanted to see Gavin now, I felt good about the two days apart. They were necessary for me to ground myself in reality. I was able to step back and try to see things objectively. But that didn't stop me from missing him.

I was trying hard to see him as he was and not as I wished him to be but the truth was the truth. He was my actual rescuer- my real knight. The thought sent shivers of delight up my spine. I suppose the same could be said for Patrick though since he did rescue me as well. Good Lord! I actually was a damsel in distress. How the hell did I get so incapable? I mean, this was a great story and all: The once capable Rebecca, is rescued by the handsome man on a motorcycle. But seriously, to have it happen for real was a bit much.

I pulled out my phone to text Gavin and there was a text from him with another photo. No rabbit this time. Just a goofy smile and accompanying text that said. "Miss you." I texted, him that I missed him too, and put my phone away. I'm not gonna lie. I was extremely glad he was thinking of me, as well.

Chapter 13

To Patrick, this deluge was a normal occurrence. It was often rainy in the Highlands. The windshield wipers whisked the water off the glass with a comforting rhythm and allowed Patrick to see the road for a split-second at each pass. Ahead of him was a narrow wooden bridge spanning a very swollen river. He started across it.

Rebecca seemed a bit nervous. "Are you sure you can see where you're going? And, are you sure you should be crossing that bridge?" The bridge was already covered by two inches of water.

Patrick shook his head. "It's the only way to get to the house, Pet."

During the drive, he had been formulating a plan to stick it to Gavin once and for all. He was glad to see that he would be able to cross the bridge after all. The water level was a bit higher than he was comfortable with but it was passable. When it rained like it was now, the river would rise several feet and cover the bridge to make it dangerous and impassible. There was a footbridge further downstream which had been raised last year to accommodate the rising water but no cars could traverse that, and the estate was too far out for anyone to walk to town at night. They would most likely have to stay the night, which he didn't particularly like to do but he would *take it on the chin*, this time.

Patrick didn't know how deep Rebecca's feelings for Gavin went or if they were reciprocated by Gavin, but he had to hope.

Patrick knew in his heart that this thing he was about to do to Gavin was very wrong but he didn't care. He and Gavin had been the best of friends all throughout childhood. Sure, things got a bit rocky during their last year together at Eton, but they got through it. It was well established that it was Patrick's idea to start a bookie ring at Eton, so the logical answer when they were discovered, was that Patrick should take the blame for all of it and not name Gavin as being involved. That way, Gavin could stay at Eton.

Patrick was perfectly happy to take the blame because he hated being stuck at Eton anyway. Getting kicked out was as much for his own sake as it was for Gavin's. In truth, he was relieved. But Gavin still carried around the guilt of letting Patrick take the blame for him. Patrick was over it but never hesitated to use that guilt against Gavin when the need arose.

Patrick's issue with Gavin began when Gavin started dating Emma. Patrick was in love with her and shared this fact with Gavin. Patrick assumed that Gavin would break up with Emma out of honor for their friendship or more importantly out of their bond of brotherhood, but that didn't happen. Eventually, Gavin got engaged to Emma and as far as Patrick was concerned, that was the end of the friendship between them.

Patrick was a master of getting people to owe him favors, and since Eton, Patrick knew that Gavin felt he owed him, but it was clear that Gavin's debt of gratitude didn't extend as far as Patrick had thought it would. When Gavin didn't break it off with her, Patrick insisted, but Gavin said he "loved her and she loves me so why would I break up with her?"

"Because we are brothers and because you owe me."

"I do owe you for a debt that I may never be able to repay, but if we are brothers you would never ask me to do what you are asking me to do."

And that was that. They were cordial to each other when they needed to be but generally, they tried to avoid one another's company.

Unbeknownst to Gavin, Patrick managed to plant seeds of discontentment about Scotland into Emma's head every opportunity he had. Whether it was his meddling that eventually led to Emma's and Gavin's breakup, he didn't know, and he didn't care. The end result was that Emma was gone and neither one of them would have her.

But if Patrick couldn't be happy, neither could Gavin, and he wanted to be the one to burst Gavin's bubble.

He felt a little bad about hurting Rebecca because she seemed to be a genuinely nice person, but she was a means to an end, and he didn't let little things like kindness or friendship stop him from getting what he wanted.

Between swipes of the wiper blades, Rebecca could see a gray, rock-walled castle with pointed spires that resembled the "It's a Small World" castle at Disneyland. It was huge. She had never been this close to such a big house in her life. Although to call this place a house was an understatement.

"This is someone's home?"

"Aye. The Laird is a bit of an odd duck. My father worked for them until he passed and now I do the odd job for them if I have the time. His son and I went to Eton together for a year or two."

Patrick parked the van in front of the huge, wooden double doors. "Well then. This rain is only going to get worse. Shall we?"

"I'll wait in the car."

"Probably the only time you'll get to see the inside of an actual castle." Patrick looked distracted as he scanned the parking area in front of the estate. He was disappointed to see that neither Gavin's motorcycle nor his car was in their usual spots near the front door.

"What's wrong?"

"Nothing." Everything. This plan of his would only work if Gavin were here. He needed to see the look in his eye. Gavin needed to see that Rebecca was with him. Patrick needed Gavin to suffer like he had. But it didn't look like he was here.

"You know, Pet. I could really use some help carrying the boxes in." Patrick nodded toward the van. "So, are you gonna help me?"

Rebecca breathed out in a playful huff. "Fine." She put her hair in a ponytail and hopped out the door after Patrick. In truth, she really did want to see the inside of one of these houses. She was an avid PBS watcher and Masterpiece Theatre was totally her thing.

She followed Patrick to the back of the van, and he placed a medium-sized box in her arms. He pointed toward the front door. "I'll be right behind you."

Patrick scanned the property one last time to see if he could find any sign that Gavin was there. He didn't seem to be.

Rebecca entered the large oval foyer, which was girded by two sets of thick, dark wooden staircases that curved to match the shape of the room. She stood in awe at the beauty before her. The dark-paneled walls were covered with paintings Rebecca guessed were the ancestors of the family that lived here. Armaments, a coat of arms, stag heads and antlers took up the remaining spaces between the paintings. Part of the wall next to the door that looked like it led to the study, had fallen off and was laying in bits near the door but other than that, the place looked to be in good condition - although, what did she know? She'd never actually been in one of these huge houses before.

Patrick entered with a load of boxes in his arms and directed her with a nod to the opposite side of the room. "Kitchen's to the right."

She took a final glance at the walls. "Do they hang everything they kill on the walls?" She backed into the quaint, warm kitchen and slammed into a sturdy woman who smelled of cake...

"No dearie. Most things we bury where no one'll ever find 'em."

Rebecca had to admit, she was terrified. After what Lacy had said, she was sure this could quite possibly be the last day of her life. She turned slowly, fully expecting to see a heinously disfigured woman holding a butcher's knife. But instead, she saw the sweetest looking, cherub-faced woman in her mid-sixties, complete with a toothy grin and a bit of flour on her nose.

The woman's countenance changed though the moment she saw Rebecca's face. She just stared at Rebecca until Patrick interrupted her with introductions. Patrick placed his boxes on the large butcher-block table in the center of the kitchen and relieved Rebecca of her load. "Rebecca, this is Beatrice; Estate Manager and cook extraordinaire. Beatrice, this is Rebecca...a lost American."

Alarm bells were ringing in Rebecca's head. The letter that started her entire adventure to Scotland, was signed by a woman called Beatrice- who also happened to be an estate manager somewhere.

She opened her mouth to question Beatrice but was interrupted by a very handsome man in his late sixties who burst through the door into the kitchen. He was accompanied by a beautiful chocolate lab who growled at Rebecca the minute it became aware of her presence.

"I shot like a bloody idiot today!" The man set his gun and a brace of grouse on the table next to the boxes. "Couldn't hit the side of a..."

The dog growled again..."Shut up, Biscuit!...The side of a barn door...Damn dog was useless today."

The man looked at Rebecca apologetically. "She doesn't fancy strangers. She's actually quite gentle when you get to know her." He patted the dog on the head. "What did you say your name was?"

Rebecca thrust out her hand, which Biscuit very much objected to, and managed to say her name with more confidence than she felt. "Rebecca Byrd."

The man didn't take her hand. He looked at Beatrice who was still visibly disturbed and then stared at Rebecca. "Good Lord!" After staring at Rebecca for an uncomfortably long time he broke the silence. "How is it that you're here?"

"I came with Patrick." She looked toward her new friend for support and he nodded his confirmation. She was so confused. There was something going on here that she didn't fully understand and she felt like she was at the center of it.

Patrick was ecstatic. This was turning out to be better than he had hoped. Clearly, everyone knew who she was, except Gavin. He still wasn't sure when he would break the news to him but he would play the innocent until the time came.

Rebecca was still being stared at quite unflinchingly and she wondered if they truly disliked Americans in the Highlands. She was just about to offer to leave the premises forever and apologize for intruding but Beatrice spoke first. "Patrick, how do ye know each other?"

Patrick smirked. "I picked her up on the side of the road."

Rebecca shrug-nodded, wishing it weren't true.

The door crashed open and Gavin, of all people, entered. Damn he was hot. He was soaked to the bone. "Main bridge is washed out again. Had to cross the foot bridge." He plopped his helmet on the table and removed his jacket, his muscles rippled under his shirt, and Rebecca couldn't stop staring. Then he saw her…"Becca? What are you doing here?"

Beatrice shook her head thoughtfully. "Ye know Rebecca?"

Gavin stepped toward her and caressed her arm gently. Rebecca couldn't take her eyes off of him. "Aye. I picked her up on the side of the road." Beatrice could almost feel the electricity between Gavin and Rebecca from where she was standing.

The back door of the kitchen burst open admitting a person covered in mud, also soaked to the bone. "The bridge is a goner 'till I can mend the dam. No-one's going anywhere tonight." His bright eyes shone through his dripping wet hair which peeked out from under a large-brimmed hat.

Beatrice kissed the muddy man on the cheek. "Braeden, Luv…could ya at least pretend to wipe the mud off your feet before entering the kitchen?" She pushed him toward the door.

"Aye, Pet. I'll do my best." His eyes locked on Rebecca for a moment, then they focused on Patrick. "Patrick, I could use your help as well."

"Sure. I'll need to get this lass sorted first." He put his arm around Rebecca as though she were his possession.

Gavin stared daggers at him. "How do you know Rebecca?"

Before she could tell Gavin that Patrick was only an acquaintance, Braeden whistled through his teeth and looked quizzically at Beatrice. "That's Rebecca?"

Beatrice nodded and turned to stare at Rebecca along with the rest of the group.

Rebecca removed Patrick's arm and inched closer to Gavin. Everyone was quiet…except Biscuit who bared her teeth at Rebecca and growled. Braeden shot a look at Beatrice who ushered the dog into the other room.

Gavin looked around the room. "Can someone please tell me what the hell is going on here?"

Beatrice took a deep breath. "Gavin, this is Rebecca Byrd…"

"Aye. I know…" Gavin placed a possessive hand on the small of her back and smiled sweetly at her. Rebecca smiled back and leaned into his warmth.

The man took a step toward Rebecca. "Rebecca, I am Lord James Gavin Alistair McDermott the Third… your father."

Gavin was utterly confused. "Father?"

James nodded. "Yes indeed…So this makes Rebecca your…"

"Sister!" Patrick burst out laughing at the revelation.

James glared at Beatrice.

Rebecca and Gavin broke their contact and stared at each other in mortification.

Beatrice looked at the wall clock…"Oh dear, look at the time, would ye? I'd better go round up the staff. We've so many rooms to ready."

James shook his head and pointed Beatrice toward the door. "Library…now!"

Beatrice shot Braeden an *oh shit* look and followed the Laird out the door.

Braeden let out a long-held breath in the form of a whistle. "I surely dunna wanna to know what kind of trouble that woman has gotten herself into this time."

Patrick, who was still laughing, glared at Gavin. He was clearly taking the opportunity to piss Gavin off. And it worked. Gavin shoved Patrick back against the wall. "You knew? You knew Rebecca was my sister?"

Patrick beamed with maliciousness. "Aye, *mate.*"

Braeden grabbed Patrick's arm and yanked him toward the back door. "Well, come on, Patrick. Let's go fix that damn dam."

Patrick placed a heavy hand on Gavin's shoulder and leaned in to whisper, "Maybe we will be brothers soon." Patrick winked at Rebecca just before Gavin pinned Patrick into the wall with his forearm. "Get out! I don't want to see you sniffing about."

And that left Gavin and Rebecca alone.

Chapter 14

A myriad of emotions rolled off of both of us in waves as we stood stock still in the thick silence of the room, neither one of us daring to look at the other. This would absolutely be considered the most colossally awkward situation I had been in in my life –ever. Not only was I *still* attracted to this guy standing before me, I sensed he was attracted to me as well. I NEVER saw this coming…ever. And I highly doubt Gavin did either. What were the odds that I would end up at the house of my "not" sperm-donor father who just happened to be the father of the guy I nearly had sex with?

Truth be told, I felt sick to my stomach. In addition to discovering that the person I was unbelievably attracted to happened to be my brother; I met my father in the absolute worst scenario possible and he looked less than enthused to see me standing in his kitchen. Also, I know everyone in there caught the obvious attraction between Gavin and me, which probably grossed James and everyone else out. Oh. My. Gosh!

And, James didn't seem to know anything about me being invited to meet him in Scotland, which made everything that much worse. What if he didn't want to meet me after all? Would he ever want to see me again? And now, to top it all off, I was stranded here overnight in this massive house. I thought about jogging back to my cottage through the rain but I had no idea where I was…again.

I turned toward Gavin. His beauty was enhanced by the depth of his stare. He was piercing me with emotions which mimicked my own. Confusion, desire, anger…mostly desire. Maybe we could move to Arkansas where no one would care?

Gavin was the first one to break the silence, addressing the least conspicuous elephant in the room. "Why Patrick?"

The pain in his face went far beyond finding out that we were siblings. It seemed like there was a history between Patrick and him that I knew nothing about. "Nothing happened between Patrick and me. I got lost on the way to the pub and he picked me up."

"You appear to get rescued a lot."

"It does seem that way doesn't it? Listen," I touched his hand in comfort (probably more for me than for him) and immediately retracted it at the realization of our newly-discovered siblinghood. I didn't finish what I wanted to say because it wouldn't make a difference now. I wanted to tell him that Patrick meant nothing to me because I really liked Gavin. A lot. But now just didn't seem to be the right time. No, check that…It would *never* be the right time. I was heartbroken. This is exactly why I kept my heart protected. The problem is, I propped it wide open for Gavin the first day I met him and now, everything just ached that much worse.

Gavin and I stared at each other in silence; neither one of us knowing what could possibly be said to alleviate the awkwardness that filled the room. He turned and retreated into the pantry. I just stood in place, afraid that if I moved, I'd break. Moments later, he returned, holding up a bottle of whiskey. "I'm sorry, we're out of Benadryl."

The tension of the last few minutes broke with my hysterical, uncontrollable laugh-cry.

Gavin stared at me, motionless, holding the bottle of whiskey in one hand and the two shot glasses in the other and then he broke into laughter as well. After we had both calmed down, we drank to the Greeks then he showed me where I would be sleeping for the night.

We lingered at the door of my room. Neither of us were sure what to say so we didn't say anything. We just stared at each other. The strong pull between us was still there- we both knew it, and we were both very confused by it.

I did the only thing I could do to break the tension. I stepped into the huge room complete with a king-sized four-poster bed and canopy and shut the door between us. Without taking a step further into the room, I sank down to the floor and wept for my breaking soul.

"Rebecca?" The concern in Gavin's voice was tangible. I knew he was dealing with a similar heartbreak but I couldn't talk about it, or to him, at the moment.

The only thing I could voice was, "Processing."

I heard him slide to the floor on the other side of the door. "Fair enough." Was all he said and we both stayed like that for a while, with a huge wall separating us.

Chapter 15

James didn't release Beatrice's arm until he had closed the door of the library. He turned to her, his eyes dark and full of emotion. "How dare you contact her without my permission! I would have contacted her myself. I just needed a bit more time."

"A bit more time. Ye've had three months…And, ye've had a heart-attack."

"Heart attack? It was a bout of angina!"

"That's beside the point." Beatrice knew she escalated the issue of the Laird's angina into something more than it was but she was thrilled that Rebecca came. In all fairness, the letter said that the Laird *may have had a bit of a heart attack*, so technically, it wasn't a lie. But the effect was the same. Rebecca was here and James had to face it.

"The point is…it was not your place to contact her."

Beatrice walked to the liquor cabinet and poured herself a shot of whiskey, which she immediately downed. "Not my place?! Ach! If I didna send her that letter ye'd never've met the girl." She poured two more shots, drank one and handed the other to James.

He nodded his thanks. "That's entirely unfair! I might have…You know what? It's none of your business."

Before James could down his shot, Beatrice snatched it from his hand and drank it, punctuating her disapproval by slamming the shot glass on the table. "Is that so? It was a different story altogether when ye left me to raise wee Gavin thirty-five years ago."

"Alright…Alright." James was three shots behind and wanted to get at least one shot down before Beatrice had finished the last of the bottle. He poured himself one and held on to the bottle. "Let's not forget I was in Kenya."

"Mmmm. Aye, it was much easier to sign up for another stint in the army than to raise yer own child."

"Well, Gavin isn't actually my child, now is he?"

"He is very much your child."

"Not biologically. His mother…"

Beatrice snatched the flask from James. "Ye know Aileen was a good woman. She didna cheat on ye. There's another explanation."

James sank down in his oversized chair and shook his head. "I don't know what happened and I don't wish to think on it anymore." He took a deep breath, resigned that he was outmatched. "If you are going to continue to interfere, at least warn me first."

The door of the library flew open and Gavin made a b-line toward the two conspirators. "What the hell, Dad! You couldn't have mentioned you had a daughter?"

Gavin noticed their disparate looks. "What?"

James looked mortified wondering if Gavin overheard them, and Beatrice looked hopeful- wishing he had.

James could tell that Gavin had feelings for Rebecca, and although he didn't know Rebecca yet, he sensed that she had feelings for Gavin as well. Although there was nothing morally wrong with them being together, the admission of the fact that Gavin wasn't his biological son would open up all sorts of questions that he didn't think he'd be able to answer at this time. "How *well* do you know Rebecca, exactly?"

"How's that relevant?"

"You're my son, she's my daughter."

Beatrice forewent the shot glass and took a giant pull of whiskey directly from the flask. "This is all very Greek."

*　*　*

After everyone had cleared the room, James thought back to the events of the evening with mortification. He had behaved rather badly regarding Rebecca, so with a sudden burst of determination, he ascended the stairs to her room and knocked lightly on her door. He didn't want to wake her. In fact, he secretly hoped she was asleep because he didn't know what he would say to her if she opened the door, but he felt he needed to try to reach out all the same.

He stood outside her door for a moment and knocked again. When he didn't hear any movement inside the room, he headed back downstairs in search of Beatrice. She'd know what to say to Rebecca. She was a woman after all.

*　*　*

Rebecca thought she heard a knock at the door just as she stepped out of the shower. She paused for a moment before deciding that she imagined it and continued to towel off. But there it was again. The faintest sound of a knock.

She dressed quickly and opened the door but no one was in the hall. She assumed it was Beatrice checking on her. She really thought she could like Beatrice. Sure, it was her fault she was here, but Rebecca wasn't altogether upset about that. She was a bit hungry though, so she headed toward the kitchen to see if she could find something to stop her growling stomach.

The house was massive and Rebecca knew she was going to get lost on the way to the kitchen anyway, so she embraced that fact and decided to do a little "exploring." She wandered down the hall in the opposite direction from the way she had come just an hour ago with Gavin, and she found a narrow, nearly hidden staircase that creaked noisily with every step she took. She considered turning around and going back upstairs, but her curiosity and hunger got the better of her. At the bottom of the stairs, she found a back entrance leading directly into the pantry.

She flicked on the light and immediately spotted a bowl of beautiful red apples and grabbed one. She felt like she was doing something wrong by sneaking around scavenging for food. But after the fiasco in the kitchen earlier, she just didn't want to run into anyone yet- if ever. Her stomach won out over integrity and she poked her head into the kitchen to check for life before making a beeline to the sink to wash it.

As she took her first bite, she heard voices outside in the foyer. One of the voices sounded like James. She really didn't want to see him just yet. Everything was still so raw, so painful. She dashed back thru the pantry door leading up the small staircase but froze on the first step as a loud creak signaled her escape.

Beatrice entered the pantry moments after the voices entered the kitchen. "That's curious. I don't remember leaving this light on." And the light flicked off.

Braeden tossed her a mischievous grin. "Well, Luv. The mind's the first thing to go."

"Ach, you shut yer trap. Yer older than I am."

James paced the room, talking to no one in particular. "I really cocked things up with Rebecca." Braeden didn't remember the last time he had seen James look so conflicted. He was usually so self-assured. "This was not how I envisioned meeting my daughter for the first time."

Beatrice turned the gas on the stove and heated a pot of water for tea. "Oh?"

He didn't need any more encouragement to continue. "I would have met her at the airport. I would have shown her the grounds. Had fresh flowers put in her room."

"Of course." Beatrice had never seen James quite like this either. He was so vulnerable, so distracted.

"And then, I'd take her for a nice pub lunch, maybe a carvery."

"You've given this quite a lot of thought then?" Braeden rubbed the stubble on his chin.

"Aye. Braeden, I have." James sank into a chair. "I was waiting for the right moment to act. These things aren't easy." What he didn't say was that he was scared to death to talk to her and to get to know her. He didn't know what to expect and now that he'd laid eyes on his beautiful, intelligent daughter, he honestly had no idea what to do.

For the first time in his life, he was at a total loss. He had no plan, no way to attack this. "I really don't know what to say to her." James' eyes found the only female in the room. "You're a woman. What would you say to her?"

Beatrice covered his hand with hers. "I'd say, 'Hello. Delightful to meet you. I regret that we didn't get to meet each other earlier. I look forward to getting to know you better.'"

James didn't say a word. He just stared blankly at Beatrice.

Braeden cleared his throat. "Maybe you should ask her if she wants to go fishing."

James perked up at the mention of his favorite sport. "Aye! Now there's a thought."

Beatrice rolled her eyes at their cluelessness.

Rebecca couldn't stop the flood of tears silently trickling down her face. Her father *did* want to get to know her and she knew that even though they missed the past 30 years, they could begin a relationship now. She never, in a million years, would have expected to meet her real father and now, to see this side of him she knew that all of the fantasies she had created about who her sperm-donor-father was, could never surpass the man standing in the other room.

She wiped her cheek and turned to head back up the stairs, but heard someone open the door to the pantry and saw light seeping under the door so she froze and held her breath. She was fairly certain she would be spending the night on the staircase. It was Beatrice.

"Now James. What do ye propose to do about the fact that Gavin is no' related to Rebecca?"

Rebecca nearly let a gasp escape her but quickly stifled it.

"I propose to do nothing. And you will quit bothering me about it."

Beatrice shuffled things around on the shelves in the pantry. "Did ye no' see how he looked at the lass? And she at him? Ye are mad if ye intend on keeping those two apart."

"He *will* gain his peerage from the House of Lords before he is told anything. I will not have him without a title." James fixed his glare at Beatrice, daring her to contradict him- rather, knowing she would.

Rebecca could barely contain her sobs as she held her breath behind the closed door.

"Gavin doesna want a peerage." She poured tea into three cups.

James nodded his head in thanks and took a sip, testing the temperature. "Nonetheless, he will have one. End of discussion."

And that was it. Rebecca wasn't related to Gavin and Gavin had no idea that James wasn't his father. She barely made it to the top of the stairs before the onslaught of emotion took out her knees, and she dropped to floor.

Chapter 16

The next morning, Rebecca woke to the sound of rain…
dripping from the ceiling in her room. The ceiling looked
like it was about to crumble to the floor at any moment. She
climbed out of bed, got dressed and tried to find someone to
tell.

This time, she took the main staircase down and followed
the voices that, conveniently, led her back to the kitchen.

She stood at the open door and watched the interaction
between Beatrice, Braeden and James. They all looked very
dignified and very British. Braeden was the first who noticed
her presence. James followed Braeden's eye line. "Rebecca?"

"Oh Yeah. Sorry. I was trying to find someone to let
them know that the ceiling in my room is leaking." She looked
from one man to the other- her heart welling up with affection
for the man she hoped to have the courage to eventually call
'Dad'.

Braeden set his teacup on the table and headed for the
door. "That would be me." He looked knowingly at James.
"You'll be alright, man."

Beatrice turned her attention toward Rebecca, who was
trying to make a stealthy exit behind Braeden, and gently redi-
rected her to sit down at the large wooden table. Beatrice set a
bowl of porridge in front of Rebecca before she even realized
what was happening.

Rebecca, knowing what was in James' heart, decided to
break the awkward silence. "I'm really sorry that I just showed
up here yesterday. I literally had no idea that this was your

place when Patrick brought me." She scrunched up her face in thought, which James found adorable. "Although now that I'm thinking about it, I'm pretty sure Patrick knew. Not really sure how." She waited for a response. Nothing...So she continued. "How long have you known about this?" She gestured between them.

The realization hit James that she had just asked him a question but he was so enamored with her that he hadn't really heard anything. "Pardon?"

"This father-daughter thing...How long have you known about it?"

"Oh, right...Nearly three months."

"I just found out a week ago. What took you so long to contact me?"

"Your mother never told you?"

"No."

Braeden shook his head as he entered. "The roof is repairable. A few slates have slipped out of place. Can't believe I didn't notice that."

Beatrice tossed a comment over her shoulder. "Eyesight is one of the first things to go, Luv."

Braeden shook his head and pecked Beatrice on the cheek before heading back out. "Aren't we a pair?"

Rebecca couldn't help smiling at the beautiful love that was clearly evident between them.

Braeden gave James a pointed look on his way out. "I dunna know how we'll have the time to fix the roof along with all of the other things falling down around us this week. Many places on that roof look like they need some care."

James nodded.

Beatrice followed Braeden out. "A word first, dear?"

"Aye?" Braeden knew that look and he was very wary.

"Aye." Beatrice began her scheming in earnest. "I'm gonna need some help to keep that girl here."

"How do you propose to do that?" Beatrice raised her eyebrows. He knew he was in for trouble when she raised her eyebrows. "Surely you've nothing malicious planned."

She kissed him hard on the mouth. "Aye. Nothing malicious at all. Just get her out of that cottage she's rented. Get her out for good."

"And how do you propose I do that?"

"You'll think of something...Maybe you could ruin her plumbing. Whatever ye do, just make it look like an accident."

"Woman, I'm beating my brains against the wall every day around here trying to *fix* things before the Gathering. Now you're asking me to deliberately ruin the plumbing at the McGerry place?"

"Aye. I suppose I am."

"What could possibly go wrong?"

She smiled. "Right. I like your confidence. I'll call all the hotels in the area. Make sure they are too full for any foreigners this month."

The only thing Braeden could do was to nod his head. "I'll leave you to your manipulation."

Gavin entered the kitchen shortly after Beatrice returned. He looked worse for wear and Beatrice's heart broke for him. She didn't see any hope of James telling Gavin the truth about his parentage until Gavin relented and accepted the peerage. But he looked as though his heart would shatter into a thousand pieces before then.

Beatrice had kept her mouth shut for years but now she wasn't sure she could keep silent much longer. James was already the legal father of Gavin. He took care of the adoption order when Gavin was young, naming Gavin as the entail regardless of his bloodline. But she knew James didn't want

Gavin to have to deal with the added scrutiny or stigma associated with being a "bastard" of sorts. Thus, the peerage. That didn't make her heart beat any easier watching the conflicting emotions pass his face as he got his first glimpse of Rebecca.

Rebecca wasn't about to ruin her relationship with her father over a secret no one knew she kept, but she kept her head down not daring to look at anyone for fear that she would suddenly blurt out what James had managed to keep from Gavin his entire life. She wasn't certain what was behind it but she knew it had something to do with his getting some title.

Rebecca jumped as Ned entered with a loud bang on the door. He waved a legal looking document in front of James. "You're gonna have to deal with this at some point." He looked at the tea. "Am I too late for brekkie?"

Beatrice, always one step ahead of everyone, set a bowl of porridge in front of Ned before he finished his sentence and was rewarded with a thankful smile.

Gavin snatched the paper out of Ned's hand. "Is this from the National Trust?' He looked between Ned and James trying to discern the mood. He wanted to pursue releasing a portion of their land to the National Trust because the upkeep on all the buildings over a thousand acres was bleeding them dry, so any news to that effect would be great news. The only problem was that in the past, his father had been adamantly opposed to the scheme. Gavin's gaze settled on James. "Have you decided to finally let me pursue this?"

"No."

Gavin slammed the paper on the table. "You are determined to see that I have nothing but the clothes on my back after you're dead if you continue ignoring these things. We don't have the manpower or the funds to keep this place up."

It was for that very reason that James continued to insist on the House of Lords. It was very important to James that Gavin had a title of his own- an official peerage because things in Scotland lately seemed to be a bit in flux. The vote for Scottish independence from England in 2014 would have shaken things up significantly for all of them if it had passed. From that moment, James pressed Gavin harder and was even more eager to have Gavin safe with his own title.

If he could just keep things quiet until Gavin was announced, that would be preferable. Gavin would have complete deniability in regard to his parentage and it would be too late to take anything back. Not that they would, but James wanted the transition clean. Besides, if Gavin knew he didn't "deserve" the title, Gavin wouldn't pursue it.

The tension between the two men was so thick Rebecca didn't dare offer to help out fixing things around the estate at that moment, but she would. She was heading back to her cottage but would be more than happy to drive back and forth every day. If nothing else, that would give her the opportunity to spend more time with her father…and hopefully avoid Gavin until she could assure herself that she could keep her emotions –and her mouth- in check.

Chapter 17

Once the bridge was passable, Braeden didn't waste time setting things in motion before Rebecca left that morning. If he were to have any peace at home, he would have to make sure that Rebecca was stuck at the estate. He was friends with old McGerry, and McGerry would understand- he knew Beatrice. Braeden would end up fixing the damage himself and didn't look forward to that with everything that constantly needed to be fixed at the estate, but it couldn't be helped.

He set about creating a blockage of some sort in the old plumbing that would burst when the pressure got too high. That was as good a plan as any. It should look like an accident. If there were any chance he'd be able to avoid fixing the mess he was about to cause, McGerry needed to be able to collect on the insurance, and Braeden certainly didn't wish to have anyone pointing fingers at him regardless of what happened.

The sun would be up in a few hours, so Braeden had a bit of time. He crept through the darkness toward the cellar door behind Rebecca's cottage wearing a pair of night vision goggles in the event that there wasn't enough light from the moon. He didn't dare turn on a torch for fear of drawing the attention of the neighbors. He was safely inside before anyone knew he was there. He crossed himself. "Lord forgive me."

* * *

Rebecca had an hour to kill before she caught a ride back to her cottage this morning with Patrick. He was the last person she wanted to spend time with, but he was heading into town for supplies and could take her without much inconvenience to everyone else. Rebecca knew there was more to the story between Patrick and Gavin and she wanted to see if she could get anything more out of Patrick. But mostly, she wanted to confront and maybe kick him in the nuts just for good measure...

Patrick said he needed to finish up a few things around the estate before they could leave, so she wandered around the halls upstairs. She had asked Beatrice where she could find her father, and she told her that he, along with Braeden and Gavin and the rest of the staff were all busy around the estate preparing for an event called The Clan Gathering that would take place in less than a week. Since Rebecca was unoccupied and couldn't speak to her father or Gavin, she decided she'd look around the massive structure the McDermotts called home.

She meandered the hallways, which were adorned with beautiful paintings, she assumed were of *her* ancestors. What a trip...Her ancestors. Prior to this, she had no idea who her ancestors were, but now, suddenly, she was a part of some long-standing family she had no information about. She knew it would take time to fit in and get to know everyone, but for now, she still felt like an outsider...a foreigner.

One painting caught her eye. It was of a very young James embracing a woman with fiery red hair and brown eyes. They looked very comfortable next to each other. She assumed this was Gavin's mother. She was a tiny little thing.

She took a closer look at James. His dark auburn hair and vibrant blue eyes took her breath away. He was a very handsome man now, but was striking as a younger man. He looked to be about Rebecca's current age in the painting, so the resemblance to him was very strong...there was no denying that she looked a lot like him.

The impact of their close resemblance hit her. She really did have a father. The proof of his paternity was evident.

Now she understood Beatrice's and James's reactions when they saw her for the first time. Beatrice had known her right off, and James took a minute but he must have seen something familiar because he couldn't take his eyes off of her.

Her eyes caught sight of an incredible likeness of Gavin. It must have been completed fairly recently because he didn't look that much different from what he looked like now.

She backed up and bumped into a warm, solid form. He wrapped his arms around her to steady her and spoke warmly into her ear. "You ready to leave?" It was Patrick. She jumped out of his embrace.

"Back off."

Patrick took her irritation in stride and leaned casually against the wall- channeling James Dean "Helluva thing about Gavin."

Rebecca glared at his obvious disregard for anyone other than himself. "Yeah. About that..." Rebecca's voice grew louder and more severe with each word. "You knew James was my father and you led me straight into an ambush." She punctuated the sentence with a shove to his chest. "Why would you do that?"

He recovered and shook his head in what nearly looked like remorse. "I'm sorry things went so poorly. In truth, I'd no idea it would happen that way."

"Why did you do it?"

"I have a history with Gavin. We don't get on."

"That's obvious." She stared at him for a moment. "Why would you want to hurt these people? They obviously care for you, but yet you would purposely try to hurt Gavin and in the process, them."

"Well, when you put it that way." Patrick had always been so focused on punishing Gavin for the past he truly never thought about the collateral damage it would inflict. There really hadn't been any true damage done before but now, here was Rebecca and Braeden and Beatrice and James; who had really been closer to him than his family and…

Rebecca stepped away from him. "You need help."

"You're probably right."

Out of nowhere, Gavin grabbed Patrick's shoulder and wheeled him around. "Typical, bloody typical. I told you to quit sniffing around."

Patrick's eyes narrowed and fixed on Gavin. "We, that is, your *sister* and I, were just having a bit of a chat. Weren't we, Pet?"

Rebecca very wisely, kept her mouth shut.

Gavin shoved Patrick toward the stairs. "Don't mess with this one, man."

The glare in Patrick's eyes when he turned toward Gavin was mixed with anger and something else. Jealousy or retribution perhaps? "You don't want to start something you can't finish." Patrick shoved Gavin back and pounded down the stairs. "Rebecca, I will see you out front."

"Just gonna say goodbye to Beatrice. I'll be right there." Rebecca waited until Patrick was out of earshot then turned on Gavin. "What the hell was that?"

"Rebecca, Patrick is not a good man. He's…"

"A wide-boy. Yeah, I know. He's an asshole. I'm not an idiot." Rebecca pushed past Gavin.

She knew that Gavin was reacting out of jealousy, and she was secretly thrilled with that, but she had to get out of that place as soon as possible. She needed time to think.

Right now she was definitely not in the right frame of mind. All she wanted to do was to kiss Gavin…hard, with all of the passion she had for him that was just simmering below the surface. She wanted him to hold her and tell her that she didn't make a mistake in coming to Scotland on a whim and that everything would work out. But she couldn't...and he couldn't...and it killed her. She had to get far away from him. Thankfully, she had enough brains in her head to rent her own place for the time she was here.

Gavin watched Rebecca flee down the stairs. He was confused and angry and hurt. Rebecca was his sister...The fact that he still very much wanted to wrap his arms around her and kiss her should have bothered him more than it did, but seeing her with Patrick bothered him more than he could imagine.

They were raised as brothers and at times, fought like brothers. They had similar tastes in women, which was the cause of the majority of their disagreements growing up, but they also pushed the limits of authority together.

At Eton, gambling was grounds for immediate dismissal. Patrick didn't have as much to lose as Gavin in terms of family honor and duty and as a result, he was able to live life to the fullest wherever he went. This was a minor source of annoyance for Gavin who had the moral responsibility of the family name to contend with. When Patrick suggested that they start a small gambling ring, Gavin's initial reaction was to say no and steer clear of it, but Patrick had a way with words. He would have made a great barrister if he had applied himself toward school as much as he did toward trying to get away with not completing his assignments.

Against his better judgment, Gavin gave in to Patrick's persistence and agreed to become a bookie of sorts. Although the endeavor was very successful for a time, an entitled, disgruntled gambling addict with terrible luck by the name of Jarvis Moncrieff, told the Headmaster about their little operation, and consequently, Gavin and Patrick were called into the Headmaster's office.

Patrick knew that Gavin would suffer far more in terms of humiliation and ridicule than he would so he took the blame entirely and urged Gavin to finish out his stint at Eton. Gavin's objections fell on deaf ears, and once again, Patrick Farrell's stubbornness and logic won out.

Gavin stayed in school and Patrick left Eton for good. Patrick's father was mortified that Patrick would treat such a gift from "The Laird" so poorly that he never quite forgave Patrick and rarely spoke to him. When Patrick's father died, Patrick refused to attend the funeral.

After the death of his father, Gavin knew that Patrick was looking to find someone to blame other than himself, so his blame fell more severely on Gavin. Gavin shouldered the burden for a time, but then there was the thing with Emma. It was years ago. Gavin was over it. Neither one of them ever ventured to talk about it. They just ignored each other but Gavin could tell that Patrick was still holding resentment toward him. But to drag Rebecca into this feud was too much. Patrick had officially crossed the line.

* * *

Rebecca found Beatrice in the kitchen pulling the most wonderful smelling creation out of the oven. "Hello, Dear. Cake?"

If Patrick weren't waiting, Rebecca would have loved a taste of the beautiful cake. "Can I have a rain check? My ride is waiting. I just wanted to thank you for everything."

Beatrice sliced into the cake and Rebecca instantly regretted saying 'no.' "I know you sent me that letter, and I guess… Well, I guess I'm glad you did, even though things were super uncomfortable."

"Oh, Darlin'. You'll get to know your father. It may take a while, but you'll both learn to make room for each other."

Rebecca smiled softly as she remembered the sweet words James had spoken about her. "Also, thanks for letting me sleep over. That bed was amazing."

"Door's always open to family."

Rebecca took a step toward the door.

"Yes, it is." The voice of James was startling and soothing to Rebecca at the same time. And, he was blocking the door. There was no clean or graceful way for her to exit, so Rebecca stood there looking like a deer caught in the headlights. James didn't help matters by staring at her either. Why was she so nervous?

Beatrice could have saved them both the agony by speaking first, but she smiled inwardly and tried her best to stay out of it. After an awkward minute, James broke the silence. "Would you like to go fishing with Gavin and me?"

Beatrice rolled her eyes.

Rebecca really had no response for him. She'd never gone fishing before and she was set on her plan to avoid Gavin at least for now, which would be impossible if she went fishing with him. "You know, cast it about?"

When she caught the hope in her father's eye, she had to accept his invitation. "Sure." She would figure out how to avoid Gavin later.

"Excellent…Oh and…I look forward to getting to know you better."

Rebecca smiled at the words he repeated from Beatrice's suggestion last night. "I look forward to getting to know you as well."

Beatrice was trying her best not to laugh out loud in joy at the scene before her but one errant laugh escaped in the form of a loud cough. "Rebecca's ride is waiting."

Rebecca nodded and exited the kitchen with a huge smile.

Chapter 18

I didn't remember there being a marsh in my front yard but I wasn't entirely certain. I was only in the cottage the two nights and it had been raining quite forcefully since I left. I stepped around it and went in, tossing a cautionary comment to Patrick, who insisted that he come inside for a chat to "clear the air." Although, I assured him it was far too early for me to spend any amount of time with him at the moment, he proceeded to follow me in.

"Watch out for the giant puddle…or pond in the front yard." Patrick hopped gracefully over it.

The first thing out of his mouth was, "You don't have a telly." And out the door he went before I could respond.

I put the kettle on and was in my room changing into clean clothes when I heard the sound of plastic ripping. Patrick was in the process of removing a beautiful, brand-new 60-inch TV from its box.

"You just happened to have a television in the van with you?"

"Aye. Got it from…a friend."

"He doesn't want it?" I didn't even realize that I didn't have a *telly* since I hadn't been home all that much, but I was hopeful that I could eventually settle in over the next few days and a TV would be great to zone out and relax to. I liked the background noise when I wrote.

Patrick had the TV set up in no time, and I figured this was his way of apologizing to me for being such an ass. He smiled and packed up his tools.

"Do you have bread and cheese and milk?"

"I believe I do, yes." And then the sexy, smiling image of Gavin popped into my mind. I felt like a traitor. I was entertaining Patrick in my home with the groceries Gavin so thoughtfully brought me.

"Wait one." Patrick was off the couch and in the back of his truck before I could respond. I stood at the door and watched him walk toward me with a giant smile on his face and brand new fondue pot in his hands. I couldn't smile back at him- until he slipped and fell and landed in the mud pit.

He was sitting waist deep in the mud covered from head to toe but still beamed when he showed me that he managed to keep the new fondue pot out of the mud entirely. "Not a scratch." He looked at his state of being. "I will need a shower, though."

"Of course." I wanted to help him out of the pit but I didn't want to get covered with mud as well.

"If you're gonna stand there looking concerned you might offer to help."

"I don't want to get dirty…but I'll take the fondue pot so you can use your hands." I was enjoying seeing him like this. He seemed like a real person just for a moment. Not a broken person trying to pretend to be someone he wasn't- or whatever- I wasn't a psychologist. "Just toss it here."

"I'm not gonna just toss you this fine appliance, Pet."

"Then I guess you're on your own, *Pet.*" Patrick could see my wry smile from where he sat.

"Aye. You win." He tossed the fondue pot to me. I caught it with ease and left Patrick alone to dig himself out.

Patrick struggled onto his knees and crawled to freedom. I brought several towels for him to wipe off with, but when I saw the landslide standing on my porch in front of me, I thought better of it and began scraping the mud off of him with my bare hands.

I had my hands all over him, and he stood very still. I looked into his eyes and saw desire there and I jumped back. "I think that's as much mud as I'm gonna get off of you. Just leave your clothes outside the bathroom and I'll throw them in the wash."

I really had absolutely no idea how he moved so quickly. Suddenly, Patrick had his arms around me and was pulling me in for a kiss. Our lips nearly touched, but instead of parting my lips for him, I pushed him toward the shower. "Bathroom is tiny, shower is crap. Don't ever try something like that again."

He smiled. "I'll be waiting for you."

I wiped the residual mud off my hands onto one of the towels. "Not gonna happen."

* * *

Gavin cursed as he watched the newly applied wallpaper slip down off the wall in front of him...again. "Father!" He tossed the sponge he was using into a bucket of paste in the middle of the floor with a splash and slammed the door behind him as he left. This caused the other two strips of wallpaper to peel off the aforementioned wall.

He strode down the large curved staircase and shoved open the doors to the atrium where James was on a ladder, glazing windows.

"This house is falling apart around us." James lowered his trowel and focused on his son. "We are stretched thin, Dad. If we want to be ready for the event, we need to hire another set of hands."

James wiped the excess glazing off the window with a rag. "With what money?"

Gavin sat down on a stool opposite James. "It's either the National Trust or we open the house to the public."

The muscles in James' jaw tensed. "I'm not gonna let anyone make a damn movie in this house if that's what you're suggesting!"

Gavin smirked. He knew which buttons to push when it came to his father. "That's not the worst idea I've heard."

"There is no way in hell I'm greeting guests at the door." Biscuit, sleeping in a corner, perked his ears up and cocked his head at James. "A solution will present itself." James closed the subject by returning to work.

Gavin was about to press the subject further when Beatrice entered carrying a tray of scones and a bowl of berries and some tea.

"Perfect timing Beatrice."

James poured water over a teabag. "There was an article about Lord Dillinger and his annual MacNab challenge early next month." James went every year and hadn't gotten a MacNab yet. Perhaps he would this year. "Oh speaking of which, Beatrice, Gavin will be lunching at the Albany with Lord Dillinger tomorrow."

Beatrice nodded and turned to leave.

Gavin spoke to Beatrice but looked directly at James. "I'm not going." He turned toward Beatrice and gave her a wink. Beatrice smiled and raised her eyebrows ever so slightly to indicate that she did not wish to be in the middle of *another* disagreement between the two of them.

Beatrice had known Gavin since he was a baby and was more of a mother to him than a housekeeper. She knew that Gavin was stubborn. When he made his mind up, he couldn't be persuaded otherwise. "Right you are."

James was just as stubborn. "Dillinger is expecting you. He wants you to take a seat."

"I told you, I don't need a title." Gavin set his teacup on the side table.

James shook his head in disbelief. "Don't be daft. Everyone needs a title."

Gavin served himself a small bowl of berries. "Seems to me, the less there is to justify a traditional custom, the harder it is to get rid of it." Biscuit watched as a few blueberries rolled off of Gavin's spoon onto the floor. He snatched them up before Gavin could pick them up.

James steeled his eyes at Gavin. "Our traditions my son, are what keep us from turning into Americans."

Gavin had never wanted a title. He didn't know why his father pushed him so hard toward it. Even if he did want the title, there was too much to do around the house this week to warrant him leaving for an hour let alone a day. But he needed time to think about Rebecca, and he knew he would have time to get his head right during the long train rides to and from London. If he left, James would have to agree to hire another person to help with repairs. Sure, Beatrice had additional staff members working around the clock on the food, decorations and set-up, but he couldn't take anyone away from her. She was incredibly short-staffed as well. "Fine, you win."

James beamed with excitement. "Truly?"

"But If I go, you agree to bring on an extra set of hands… by tomorrow."

"I will look into things."

Gavin smiled and pushed a little more just to get a rise from James. "I really think we should cancel the Clan Gathering. It's less than a week away and we don't have enough…"

James glared at Gavin. "This family has kept that tradition for nearly a century."

"Custom is petrification; nothing but dynamite can dislodge it for a century."

"Stop quoting Twain."

"The truth is the truth. No matter how painful. We need to cancel…"

"No. End of discussion." And with a sip of his tea, the discussion was over.

So, they would host the Clan Gathering, and Gavin would go to the House of Lords. Gavin didn't want to follow in his father's footsteps. Sure, he loved the land and his home, but he wanted to be part of the process. He wanted to work the land, not just be a figurehead to "rule" over it all. James was of the old-school mentality, and that was fine when the estate was producing crops, but life wasn't like that anymore. People moved away and the unproductive fields were just too costly to maintain.

To help pay for the estate, Gavin purchased several bee-hives and began producing honey several years ago. Also, a few years back Gavin had the wisdom to inoculate 30 acres of their extensive forest, which was a mixture of oak, hazel, Scots pine and birch, with black truffle spores, but that was a costly investment, and they wouldn't produce for six to twelve more years. After that, the sales could yield hundreds of thousands of pounds a year, which would remove the albatross hanging around their necks, once and for all. But they needed to get rid of some of the debt now before they went under entirely. The taxes every year were sucking them dry.

Despite his stubbornness, Gavin knew that his father only wanted what was best for him, but what Gavin thought was best for himself was entirely different from what his father thought was best. Gavin wanted this old, tired mansion to be his home, not just a house.

His thoughts drifted to Rebecca and he caught himself thinking about what would have been. There was something beautiful between them even that short time. He needed to shake her.

Gavin left his father in the atrium and joined Beatrice in the kitchen where he helped himself to several sandwiches she had strategically placed on a large, silver tray. She glared playfully at him and he responded with a weak smile. But Beatrice noted, this smile was different somehow. "You look like Wullie after knocking P.C. Murdock's helmet off with his catty."

Gavin plopped another sandwich in his mouth and glared but said nothing.

"Rebecca?" The timer on the oven rang and Beatrice turned it off. Then she opened the AGA and removed a beautiful white cake. She was careful to wave it under Gavin's nose as she passed him.

Gavin shook his head. "It's Patrick. He's got no business goin' after her."

Gavin reached toward the cake to rip off a piece. His hand was promptly swatted away with a towel. "Manners." She pulled out a knife and sliced him a piece.

The door swung inward, and Braeden walked through backward, carrying a crate full of sectioned honeycomb. Gavin took the crate from him and set it on the table. Braeden nodded his thanks then reached toward the cake with his bare hand. "Did you make this for me, love?" Beatrice slapped his hand away and shook her head and sliced a second piece.

"Gavin, I do believe that my dear husband's lack of manners may have rubbed off on ye." She snatched the remaining cake off the table and moved it away from the both of them.

Braeden swatted Beatrice on her backside. "Aye. Maybe you should teach me a lesson."

She turned to face her assailant with a smirk. "I've tried. You're hopeless."

He waited until she was clear of the cake and pulled Beatrice toward him.

Gavin smiled at the playful banter that was common between Beatrice and Braeden.

"You've got that far away look about ya, son." Braeden patted him on the shoulder. "Everything alright?"

Gavin shrugged. "It will be- in time."

Braeden grabbed his cake and headed toward the door. "C'mon Gavin. Let's finish with the honey."

"Aye. I've given up on the wallpaper for now."

Braeden and Gavin climbed to the top of the small rise that overlooked the estate below. The beehives were just outside a cave perched atop a lush green pitch. The wild flowers that covered the grounds and surrounded the cave were not indigenous to the area. Gavin and Braeden had planted them several years ago in anticipation of starting a small apiary. The flowers thrived in the moist environment and now the area was covered in them and the flowers were covered with bees.

Braeden silently removed the lid of one of the beehives and began smoking the bees with an antiquated apparatus. "I found someone to help you with these bees if you'd take it." He removed three foundationless frames from inside the hive and placed them on a table situated just inside the entrance to the cave. "Although, I doubt you will."

Gavin used an equally antiquated knife to cut the combs from the frames. "Why wouldn't I?" Gavin crushed the combs into a large plastic bowl with a potato masher and Braeden poured the combs into a makeshift strainer bucket.

"Because it's Patrick."

Gavin scraped the last bit of the mashed combs out of the bowl. "Well, that one's a bloody black cloud hangin' over my head. I'd sell the place AND move to Ireland before I let myself get into his debt any further."

"I thought as much."

"I know he helps you on occasion, but there is no way I'll let that wanker handle my bees." Braeden had too much to do around the place already and for that matter, so did Gavin. They needed a full-time keeper or, ideally, someone to take over the home maintenance for Braeden on a daily basis so Braeden could focus on being a gillie when the need arose and could tend the bees full-time. Braeden was getting up there in years and Gavin had taken on more of Braeden's responsibilities around the estate but Gavin was trained in running a business, not construction. Sure, Gavin was pretty handy with power-tools or a hammer and nails, but sweating pipes or maintaining wiring and electrical components was not really his thing. He'd been nearly electrocuted one too many times.

"Son, you should deal with what is troubling you."

Gavin nodded. He knew that he and Rebecca needed to talk things through, and the sooner the better as far as he was concerned. He could only imagine what she was going through being in a strange country and meeting her father for the first time. "Braeden, I've got to see Rebecca. Gonna knock off for the day."

"Aye. Go. We're nearly finished."

Chapter 19

"Rebecca?" I heard the urgency in Patrick's voice and ran to the bedroom to find him, wrapped in a towel, standing in a puddle of water that was rapidly expanding. "I believe your pipes may have burst."

"Crap!" I ran to the linen closet and grabbed all of the towels I could find and dropped them futilely on the floor. They were soaked in moments. Then, I looked under the sink and behind the bathtub for a panel that would lead to a valve so I could turn off the deluge. "I don't see any way to turn it off!"

"Try around back. Many of these old places weren't originally plumbed. Sometimes they had to dig a cellar."

"Thanks. Oh, your clothes are in the dryer. They're dry. You should put them on."

"Thanks, Pet."

I ran around to the back of the house and saw a cellar door, went inside, dug around and finally found the valve and turned it off, but not before the entire cottage was an inch thick with water. What I wouldn't have given for my shop-vac right about now.

I entered the house and was assaulted by a horrible smell as I returned. "What is that smell?"

"It appears your sewage is also backing up."

It took all of 5 minutes for me to pack. I barely had time to unpack anything in the first place so I lucked out there. I didn't know what kind of ticking time bomb I was currently living in and I didn't want to find out, so I shoved everything in my suitcases; clean and dirty alike and, I rushed out the door, thankful for Patrick's help loading my convertible while I called every hotel and Bed and Breakfast in the area.

He saw the confusion on my face as I hung up the phone. Oddly, there wasn't a single vacancy in the entire town. The town must be hosting a convention of ghosts because there weren't enough people here to fill up the four establishments. I doubted that the hotels filled up even during high season-which this wasn't.

"It looks like I'm heading to the estate."

"You're sure you don't need help finding it?"

"I'm fine."

"You do have a lot of luggage. You won't be able to shut the top if it rains."

"I'll manage."

I knew the sensible thing would be to put my suitcases in the back of Patrick's van and have him lead me there, since it was so easy to get lost around here. But I needed to handle something by myself for a change. And I was tired of being rescued. Tired of feeling helpless, and I just wanted to get going.

I looked into the sky, willing this break in rain to hold long enough for me to get to my father's place.

The last time I showed up unannounced, I was at Patrick's mercy. This time, I wanted to step up there on my own terms. I knew they'd take me in because Beatrice had offered just this morning.

"When can I see you again?"

"I need to figure out what I'm doing."

"I'll pop round the house in a few. That should be enough time."

"That's conveniently non-specific. How about I call you when I'm ready to chat?"

I had no idea how much time it would take me to process all of this.

He kissed me sweetly on the forehead. "Shouldn't prevent you from spending time with a friend. I'll just come 'round."

"You're relentless, and we aren't really friends yet, are we? Before you answer, that was a rhetorical question."

I needed to get on the road and didn't want to stand around debating the length of time it would take me to work my stuff out. So I deflected.

"Thanks for everything. I really need to get out of here before the rain starts again." I moved in for the awkward cheek-kiss thing and went left when I should have gone right and ended up kissing Patrick on the mouth. He didn't seem to mind. But nevertheless, there we were, accidentally kissing on the front porch for the whole world to see.

* * *

Gavin slowed as he passed Rebecca's house shocked that the wanker was kissing Rebecca. He shouldn't have been surprised, though. Patrick was a dog, and he knew how to push Gavin's buttons. But he crossed the line with Rebecca. Sure there was an amazing, undeniable connection between them, and Gavin knew he would have to conquer that. He had to start thinking about her as a sister. *Half- sister* he reminded himself. But half or whole, he knew he couldn't be anything more to her than just a brother.

But Patrick would ruin her. Gavin tried to convince himself that these feelings weren't jealousy, but were just the feelings of a protective brother who didn't want to see his half-sister fall in with the wrong guy. Maybe he ought to suggest that she leave Scotland?

He was being unreasonable and he knew it. He couldn't ask her to leave just when she met her father- their father. She would want to stay. She should stay. He wanted her to stay. He could leave. But he knew he couldn't leave the area for more than a day or two so obviously, that wasn't a valid solution.

He found himself eager to hop on that train to London in a couple of days. He didn't like the reason he was going, but he was done fighting James on it. At least he would be able to avoid her and Patrick. He was really discouraged that Rebecca had moved from him so quickly. He felt a definite connection between them when they first met and was certain she felt it too, but now he wondered if that feeling was one-sided.

Gavin plowed through the door of the noisy Fox and Hen and immediately felt a little better. He loved the sounds and the smells of the old place. The same people were there who had always been there. Ewan, Kara, Old Pete…They would trickle in and out all week (except for Maggie). Maggie had her own stool. The unspoken order was that it be vacant every morning by 9am.

Ned saw the anger bubbling in Gavin's eyes and drew a dark ale on tap for him. He placed it in front of Gavin when he sat down.

"Cheers." Gavin took a long draw. "How long do you think you owe a person when you owe a person?"

"Well, we're Celts aren't we? Long memories."

"Aye. You make one poor choice and it still haunts you nearly two decades later." He finished his drink and indicated for Ned to pour him another.

"Patrick?"

"He pisses on everything, man. He's trolling after Rebecca."

Ned set the second beer on the bar. This bloke was in love. He needed to help him, but although he was one of four

123

people who knew James' secret, he was not allowed to divulge it. He'd have to think of something.

"He's like a parasite. There is nothing I can do about him. He's everywhere. He's infected every part of my life." Gavin slugged back the last bit of his beer and shook Ned's hand before leaving. "Cheers, mate. I'll think of something."

"I know you will, son. You always do."

Chapter 20

It was pouring rain by the time Rebecca finally found the estate. She was soaked to the bone, but she stood at the door unable to knock. She considered sleeping in her tiny car, but she'd already lugged her suitcases to the front door.

"Ya gonna just stand there and drip?" Hearing Gavin's deep burr so close behind her sent chills up her spine- the good kind of chills- which she immediately squelched.

"I wasn't sure if I wanted to knock."

Gavin opened the door and ushered her in. The estate was full of bustling workers setting up for some event.

"There are so many people."

"Aye." He was different; cold, angry. His eyes were dark and unsettling. "Do you think you can find your room?"

"Yes."

"I'll let Beatrice know you're here." He stared down at her. "*Why* are you here?"

"She's here because this is her home." Beatrice cuffed Gavin on the shoulder. "I thought I heard your wee voice, luv." Without ceremony, Beatrice yanked Rebecca's dripping coat off of her and hung it up on the rack of coats near the door. "Ach, ye're soaked."

"It's raining."

"Aye. That it is."

"And, I had a bit of trouble with the plumbing at my cottage."

"Did ye, now?" Beatrice's back was facing Rebecca, but she'd swear Beatrice was smiling.

"Yeah. And oddly, there are no rooms available at ANY of the hotels in the area…for a month."

"Ye don't say." Beatrice headed toward the kitchen. "Must be filled up due to the Gathering. Gavin, help the lass carry her luggage upstairs."

Neither one of them seemed comfortable with the situation. "I can do it myself. I'm sure you have other things you could be doing."

"Aye, I do. But we need to talk." Gavin grabbed her large suitcase and hefted it up the stairs. Rebecca trailed behind with her smaller cases hoping Gavin would forget about talking. The last thing she wanted to do with him was talk.

Gavin set her luggage in the room. Rebecca noticed that her ceiling had been fixed and painted. "The leak is fixed?"

"Aye. And that's not what we need to talk about." Gavin sat on the settee at the foot of her bed.

Rebecca sat across the room on a cute decorative chair. She couldn't bear to be close to him without touching him. She quietly waited for him to start.

"What's going on with you and Patrick?"

That wasn't at all what she expected "None of your business."

"I saw you kissing him in front of your house."

"What you saw wasn't what you think you saw… Creepy stalker…"

Gavin stood up and began pacing the room. "He's bad news. You need to stay away from him."

Rebecca could tell that he was very affected by her continued proximity to Patrick. He was shaking. Gavin looked heartbroken and angry at the same time, and she knew where all of this emotion was coming from. She reached out automatically in comfort and touched his shoulder. "He's just a… friend." It wasn't that she believed Patrick was really a friend per se, she hoped that statement would make things easier on him- if she assured him that there was nothing between them.

Gavin turned to her and his eyes mimicked hers again. Longing and passion. Then in a split second, his eyes returned to the previous set of hurt and confusion and he stepped away from her. "Patrick is not your friend. You should stay away from him." He spoke very quietly, which made everything that much more intense.

Before Rebecca could respond, Gavin left, shutting the door behind him.

Chapter 21

Rebecca barely slept the entire night thinking of Gavin. She paced back and forth in front of her window as she watched the sunrise wishing she could change things with him, but she couldn't. She had to respect traditions she knew nothing about. Exhausted, Rebecca flopped into one of the oversized chairs across the room from her bed and stared at the wall for a while, trying to clear her mind. When the beige flatness became uninteresting, Rebecca pulled out her notebook. Maybe spending time as Abigail, would take her mind off of Gavin.

On occasion, Abigail would ask Ciro to comb her hair with his talons because it would get very tangled after she would bathe in the lake. He was more than happy to comply and wished she would take a dip in the lake every day.

When the three days were up, Ciro announced that he would take her to where her father was himself but that for her safety, she would only agree to stay for three days.

"I don't know if that is enough time, darling Ciro. You must let me go to him and you must let me stay as long as I must."

Ciro didn't know if he was strong enough to let her go but he acquiesced. "I do not like it. I fear for your safety. There are things out there you know nothing about and I will not be able to stay close to you to help you."

"If I do need you, how will you know?"

Ciro went to the back of the cave and Abigail heard the shuffling of rocks and the sound of metal. Ciro returned with a small, very sharp knife. "Do you trust me?"

"With my life."

"Then give me your hand" Ciro sliced into the soft part of his finger and then made a small cut on the palm of Abigail's right hand. He pressed the cuts together and said something over them in a strange language Abigail didn't understand.

The cut on her palm began glowing blue like the color of Ciro's eyes and she felt very dizzy. And then everything went black but she vaguely remembered Ciro saying if she called out to him he would hear her and he would come.

And Rebecca wished that Gavin would learn the truth and call out to her. Frustrated, she moved to her window and watched a little brownish bird fly around the quaint courtyard. And then Rebecca saw Gavin.

Gavin looked up at her window and their eyes met. He continued walking toward the house and Rebecca followed him with her eyes. She knew they were both feeling the same thing. Heartache. Her heart ached for Gavin. To be fair, he was probably dealing with much stronger emotions than Rebecca was since Rebecca knew what she felt for him was acceptable. He didn't. But it was heartache nonetheless.

Rebecca needed to get out of her room. She needed to blow off some of this energy she had and wanted to help around the estate if they needed her. By the sounds coming from the rest of the house, everyone was busy working, getting ready for the big event. Rebecca stepped into the hall and immediately felt a surge of excitement. She was eager to work with her hands.

From the large balcony overlooking the foyer, Rebecca watched the staff decorate. She could only imagine how beautiful this place would be after they were through and she was glad she'd arrived in time to see it.

Rebecca found a large window on the second floor that overlooked the back *garden* as they called it. It wasn't a garden. It was a massive lawn that stretched back about 500 yards and ended in a wide river only to pick up again on the other side. And from this height, the *garden* seemed to continue for several miles. There was a fairly dense forest on one side and the other side was mostly rolling hills with a few trees. She could also see the back side of the ruins Gavin brought her to the other day. It stood as a sentinel on the hill almost exactly opposite the estate. And Rebecca knew the sea was just on the other side of that.

Rebecca could see why James didn't want to give it away to the National Trust, but she could also see Gavin's side of it, and if Rebecca were a tourist, she'd love to visit the ruins. She wondered if opening it to the public would be possible without giving it to the Trust.

Without warning, the rain began dropping in sheets, and a foggy greyness descended rapidly over the area, making it difficult for Rebecca to see much past the river. The rain didn't seem to faze anyone who was working outside. They just continued measuring plots of ground, trimming the grass near the river and painting the beautiful gazebo. Rebecca knew they shouldn't paint in the rain but maybe the U.S. had different paint standards than they did here in Scotland?

Before she could decide which direction to go, she heard a string of cursing traveling down the hallway and followed it until she found Gavin in one of the upper rooms, hands on his hips staring at the wallpaper which was slowly sliding down the wall. Rebecca imagined him as a small child, standing like that when things didn't go his way and Rebecca let out a quiet laugh.

Gavin scowled at her. He wasn't in the mood. He had two days to get three more rooms, plus a slew of other things ready before the Gathering and just couldn't be bothered. Especially not by Rebecca. She still consumed nearly every waking thought and he needed to keep some distance between them. For both of their sakes. He felt the energy pass between them this morning when they found each other through the window. He was certain she felt it too.

"Are you using wheat paste?"

"What?" He snapped at her. He didn't know what she was talking about and really had no time for interruptions. He needed to find Braeden and get his input on what to do with these old walls.

Rebecca could hear the exasperation in Gavin's voice and she didn't want to drag this out any longer than need be so she inspected the paste herself.

It was lumpy, just as she had expected.

"Do you have a strainer?"

"No."

Rebecca rolled up her sleeves and drove her hands into the lumpy paste. "You have to get the lumps out first."

Gavin just stood there. His mind was blank. She was mesmerizing. He loved watching the way her graceful fingers mixed through the paste. He watched that one stray curl come untucked from behind her ear, and he tucked it back behind her ear for her. The smile she gave him melted his heart, and he smiled back- holding her gaze.

"Thanks."

He hadn't slept much in the past few days so it took him longer than it should have to realize that he shouldn't have touched her or looked at her that way.

Her voice brought him back to reality. "Are you gonna help me or just stand there?"

He dunked his hands in the bucket and helped Rebecca mix.

Rebecca took her hands out of the mixture and shook them gently to get some of the paste off, but in doing so, several globs of the paste ended up on Gavin's face. Gavin's look of shock at getting splashed with paste changed immediately to a wide grin and before she knew it, the side of her face was on the receiving end of a massive handful of goo. And then… it was on.

"Ah. Rebecca. Beatrice said you were here." They both jumped at his voice and simultaneously, dropped the globs of paste they still held, to the floor like two children caught with their hands in the cookie jar.

James didn't seem to notice the paste covering them as well as the floor and subsequent walls. "Getting along I see."

Biscuit growled at Rebecca, and James continued staring at the two of them, seemingly deep in thought.

"Well, come along, Biscuit." James walked down the hall, and Biscuit growled one last time as if to make a point before he followed. "F'god sake Biscuit, shut up. She's my daughter."

Rebecca shook her head. "Can't imagine things not ever being weird around him."

"The dog?"

"The dad."

"I think he'll come around too."

"I agree."

Gavin nodded to the wall. "Shall we?"

Rebecca picked up the paste bucket. "We don't have any paste left…"

Gavin, Cheshire Cat grin across his face, scooped a wad of paste from the top of Rebecca's shoulder and smeared it on the wall. Rebecca found a few mounds on the floor and soon, the job was done. The wallpaper stuck to the wall but the room needed a good steam cleaning- so did both Gavin and Rebecca.

Chapter 22

Rebecca was hungry. James and Beatrice made it very clear that this was now her home and Rebecca was to do whatever she liked to without permission. Beatrice had also explained that normally she fed the family at set hours but this week, while they were prepping for the Gathering, it was "every one for themselves." She knew she didn't need permission to scrounge around in the kitchen but she still felt a lot like an intruder. The fact that she didn't know where anything was certainly didn't help, so when James entered the kitchen after her, she was relieved, and a little embarrassed.

James smiled at her and sliced two thick pieces of bread, dropped them into the toaster and turned on a kettle of water.

"I was going to have a bit of a nosh before bed. Care for some tea?"

She nodded and followed his gesture to be seated. "That would be great."

"Beans on toast?"

Rebecca let out a sigh of relief. "Oh my gosh. Yes, please."

James puttered around the kitchen in relative silence and Rebecca watched. This was her father. Her blood. He was real. She had created so many scenarios about who he was over the course of her life that it was hard for her to grasp that James was an actual person. Most of her fabrications about her father revolved around him being an FBI or CIA agent who saved the world.

She nearly laughed out loud at the difference between her fantasy father and the comforting mundaneness of the reality she was looking at right now. He was peaceful, secure, safe. He was real and tangible, and she was a part of him.

After a few minutes of bustling around the kitchen, James set a cup of tea and a thick piece of toast loaded with beans in front of her, and he sat opposite her.

"Thank you." Rebecca beamed at him and James felt as though his heart would burst with love for this beautiful child he was finally able to get to know. She would have to learn how to make a proper cup of tea though. James stopped Rebecca from removing her teabag. "Give it a minute to steep, Lass. It's not ready yet."

"Alright." She put the teabag back.

Out of the blue, Biscuit nudged her. Rebecca looked up at James with the most endearing and joyful look on her face.

"If you feed him, you'll never get rid of him."

Rebecca smiled at the canine and slipped him a bit of her toast. She was rewarded with a lick a few moments later. "Well, that sure beats the growling." Rebecca scratched Biscuit on the head.

"He'll never leave you alone, now." James tossed a piece of his toast to the dog and smiled warmly at Rebecca.

"Yes, well Biscuit is irresistible."

"That he is." He tucked into his beans. "I hear you're a writer. Have I seen your work?"

"I sure hope not." She'd be mortified if James ever read any of the books she'd written. She didn't even know if she'd ever get around to finishing the one she was working on now, but if she did, she'd probably let him read that.

"Are you working on anything now?

"Yes. It's kind of a fairy tale. I haven't had a lot of time to work on it lately."

James removed his tea bag and indicated that Rebecca should do the same. "Sometimes the best things are ready in their own time. If we try to force them, they turn into something entirely different. Like tea."

He was deep. Rebecca had a feeling that he wasn't just talking about the tea. He was talking about their relationship. He knew, like she did, that it would take them both a little while to adjust to the changes. He understood that she was in an odd place in her life, and he was giving her an inclination that he was in a similar place as well.

"Fishing tomorrow?"

"Sounds fun."

"Gavin will see that you have appropriate gear."

"Great." She watched this ordinary man eat his ordinary food and was more at peace in that moment than she had been in a long time. "I've always wondered what makes fishing so special to people?"

"Many men go fishing all of their lives without knowing that it is not fish they are after."

"Quoting Thoreau?"

"You know him?"

"Not personally." She returned his laugh with a smile.

"Well, I should say not."

"English Lit major."

"Ah. So what do you think he meant by that then?" He finished his tea and stood to grab the kettle. He held it up to her. "More tea?"

"Yes. Thank you." She thought on it a moment. "I think it has to do with never being happy right where you are and always looking for the next best thing. You know, 'the grass is always greener on the other side.'" Rebecca stopped short. "Until recently, it never occurred to me that I was living in a skewed sense of the future and not living in the present."

James nodded thoughtfully. "I think we all are guilty of that from time to time." James patted Rebecca gently on the hand. "So you see, fishing turns us all into philosophers. That's what makes fishing special."

Rebecca laughed.

They ate their beans and toast and drank their tea, and their time together wasn't as awkward as Rebecca had thought it would be. This was OK. This was just the beginning. Things would get better from here. There was hope.

Chapter 23

It was a beautiful morning. Actually, beautiful didn't even begin to describe it. Idyllic maybe? Surreal? From where I was standing, crotch-deep near the bank of the swollen river, I felt like I was in Hobbiton or some sort of fairyland.

The rain had stopped and the pink and gold light of the sunrise caught every bead of mist rising from the river, casting a surreal lime-green glow over the fields. Each droplet of mist was its own unique prism, and I just stood there in the midst of it, totally mesmerized. I was literally fishing at the base of a rainbow.

It was so quiet, so peaceful. I had never experienced such an absence of sound in my life. Sure, I could hear the river and I could hear a few birds now that the sun was rising, but there were no sounds of cars or technology anywhere. It was amazing.

I had moments of relative silence in Santa Barbara, when standing on the beach at the ocean watching the birds diving into the waves and humpback whales migrating or dolphins frolicking in the water. Those sounds were beautiful, but they all mixed together. But here, the sounds seemed individual. Separate. Distinct somehow. It was perfection.

I had never gone fly fishing before, and although I thought I was getting the hang of it, clearly the hook in my hair told another story. Gavin had to retrieve the lure, or fly, or whatever they called it, from my hair on numerous occasions. I was really trying my best to cast; I just couldn't get the rhythm right. The waders were surprisingly warm though but

I was worried that I would tear mine on a rogue branch or something so I tried not to move a whole lot.

When we first arrived at the river, James was very attentive and took care to find me the perfect place to stand where I would be "able to steer clear of the trees should you need to re-cast." After he got me sufficiently settled, he pointed upstream about 100 yards. "I'll be just there if you should need me." I think he just wanted to keep an eye on me, which I thought was wonderful.

I nodded my thanks to him after he cast my line for my first go 'round and Gavin and I shared a silent laugh at my expense because the moment James set himself upstream, my line caught on a stray bit of wood floating past my hook.

I removed the wood and tried to cast by myself by trying to mimic James and Gavin, but the hook snagged in the tall grass behind me: And then it briefly found Biscuit, whose yelp was quite dramatic. (I fully anticipate more growling in our futures.) And then finally, it got stuck in my hair. It wasn't all horrible. I did manage to get it in the water a time or two as well. Over the course of a few hours, my skills did improve.

I had been instructed by my father that there was to be "a limited amount of talking. We don't wish to scare the fish off." So I finally mouthed "help me" to Gavin and he gave me that adorable half smile taking pity on me.

He reached for my fishing pole and helped me cast it… exactly like one of those golf or baseball movies where the sexy man steps up behind the heroine and talks low in her ear and says "let me help you," but what he really means is "let's have sex after I wrap my manly arms around you and pretend to teach you how to perform this task just so I can touch you" and then he trails soft kisses down her neck…" except Gavin didn't wrap his arms around me or whisper or anything. He just stood next to me and grabbed the reel and cast the line beautifully in the water then handed it back to me with a wink. Sometimes fantasy does trump reality.

He moved a good 100 yards away downstream and cast his own line into the water.

I didn't bother trying to cast again. So I stood there forever and I watched the water ripple downstream, checked my fingernails and determined that I was in desperate need of a manicure. And then I watched the river some more. Then my line jerked, and I nearly lost my pole.

"I think I caught something." I yelled and sure enough there was a huge salmon, fighting on the end of my line. This was surely the dumbest salmon on the planet. I wasn't "teasing the fish with the fly" as James put it. And there was no bait on the line. So unless that fish was occupied in thought and ran head-long into the hook, I had to assume it was mentally deficient somehow.

"Gavin, help her reel it in." James waded toward me as fast as he could

And Gavin helped me. He didn't take the pole from me. He let me have the experience of reeling it in but he did wrap his arms around me. More out of necessity than pleasure. He grabbed the pole in one hand to secure it and helped me turn the crank with the other.

Now, I'm a very strong person but Atlantic Salmon can get up to 100 pounds and nearly 5 feet in length or as Gavin told me earlier "46 kilograms and 150 centimeters." That would literally be like hauling in one of those Hollywood actresses while she kicked and fought against the line trying to swim in another direction. There was no way I could do this myself.

Strange comparison I know.

It's not that I spend my time hanging out with actresses, but I had the opportunity a few years back to spend some time with one Hollywood actress on a train from Santa Barbara to Burbank, and we chatted for a bit to pass the time. She was a swimmer and runner and a writer and a mother, as well as an actress. She was truly beautiful and had the most amazing spirit and was incredibly tenacious and hilarious. But she was literally the most petite person I had ever seen in my life, so when I saw that fish exiting the water, I thought of her. A fighter. This salmon turned out to be nearly 60 pounds. I couldn't believe it.

So, as much as I would have loved to revel in the closeness of Gavin's body pressed up against mine, I didn't. I was entirely focused on hauling that giant, fighting beast out of the water, against the current. My arms were burning and my hands were cramping, and this act of catching a fish became so much more in that moment. It was confirmation that if I just held on a little longer, things would all work out. In life. And with this fish. I tightened my grip on the pole and cranked with all my might: For the time lost getting to know my father, and for Gavin and for my mother and most importantly, for myself.

And so, we had salmon for lunch. And it was amazing.

Apparently, according to James, I was the only one who had caught a salmon in over 6 months. "Salmon are wiley little buggers, and that's what makes the MacNab so competitive."

I looked from Gavin to James and back again. "What's a MacNab?"

James almost seemed put off that I didn't know what a MacNab was, and I was about to state the obvious, that "I'm an American," but then, with a pat on my hand, he smiled and explained the MacNab to me.

"One must stalk a red deer, shoot a brace of grouse and catch a salmon all in one day." He paused to let the enormity of the task set in.

I knew how hard it was to reel in that fish so I understood at least part of the epic challenge but I had another question. "Does the deer need to be red?" Silence. They both just stared at me like I had three heads. "I mean, can you shoot a brown deer, or a beige one or do you have to find a red one?" Still nothing.

Thankfully, Beatrice had taken a moment to eat with us. "A Scottish red deer is just a type of deer that is native to the Highlands." Come to think of it, I don't remember Beatrice ever sitting down, let alone eating. That woman was going all the time.

Anyway, both James and Gavin seemed accepting of her explanation- I saw them nod.

"Ah ok, got ya."

After another brief silence brought on by the fabulous berry pie Beatrice served with ice cream, James looked directly at me. "How do you find your...accommodations?"

"They're amazing. My room here is probably bigger than my home in the States."

"Oh...well...I rather hoped you would think of this as your home."

The look on his face was so endearing I had no response. I was so touched by what he had offered and I didn't want to cry right there in my pie. "Oh...well...uh...Thank you. I'd like that."

He smiled at my answer and then after a moment, turned to Gavin. "Gavin, you are all set to meet with Dillinger tomorrow. You should have your appointment with the House end of this week if all goes well." I was mesmerized by the rich, deep timbre of his voice. This was the voice of the man who made up half of my genes. I couldn't believe I was in the same room with him. My father...

Gavin, clearly accustomed to James' presence, responded with exasperation. "I really don't want to have anything to do with those people."

"Son, I am those people."

"I can't take the time away this week. There are too many repairs. And I don't need a title."

Since I knew that Gavin getting a title was the only way that James would divulge his paternity, I was more than happy to give him my two cents. "I definitely think you should get it. And the sooner the better." The statement may have come out a bit more forceful than it should have. Everyone looked at me oddly, and Gavin seemed really angry.

"Well, thank you all for deciding what is best for me." Gavin stood abruptly. "I'm gonna start on the floor of the atrium."

"I can help out." I really could. This would be a dream. If I had to stay here at the estate, then I might as well use my awesome fix-it skills on something other than *build a birdhouse* day at Boltz Hardware.

James looked unconvinced.

"What? I'm good at that kind of stuff."

Gavin nodded. "Well, she knew what to do with the paste." He turned to me. "It would be terrific if you are up for it."

"Of course I'm up for it! I've always wanted to 'ply my trade' on a worthy fixer upper. And this is a way better use of my time than working on the crack house I was originally looking at."

Gavin looked quizzically at me. "Crack house?"

"Not important."

James stood. "It's decided then. You two get started. And Gavin, you will take that meeting with Dillinger."

Chapter 24

Gavin absently wiped the grout off of the floor tiles with a sponge. He was paying more attention to Rebecca than he was to the floor, and the floor was suffering for it. She really did look like their father. He began to think that maybe his instant closeness with her was due to that. She raised an eyebrow at him. She must've sensed him looking at her.

He tried to cover the awkwardness with nonchalance. "I'm gonna tackle the rock wall near the gazebo after we finish this floor. How are you with mortar?"

"Insanely good."

"Roofing?"

"Absolutely."

"Glazing windows?"

"Please…" Glazing widows was like caulking a bathtub. Even her mother could glaze a window.

"Sweating pipes?"

"Child's play."

Gavin sat back on his heels. "Who are you?"

Rebecca didn't think Gavin realized what a loaded question that was. Just over a week ago, she flew to Scotland to meet her father, discovered she had a "people," saw men in kilts in real life and found out that she had an ancestral home…She left everything she was familiar with behind. So, although his question was meant to be rhetorical, she really couldn't have answered it even if she'd wanted to.

The floor of the atrium was nearly finished. They had been working non-stop since they started and had already repaired the wallpaper in two additional rooms- and managed to keep the paste in the bucket or on the wall. They would be finished with this floor tonight, which would give them one more day to complete an unending list of repairs before the Clan Gathering on Saturday.

"What is the Clan Gathering exactly?"

"Well, it's a three-day event, actually a three-day excuse for all of the families in the area to join together and drink until stupid then they go hunting and fishing... The MacNab, you remember."

She nodded.

"It's a tragedy waiting to happen, really."

She smiled at the image. "Other than mass mayhem, is there anything else to look forward to? You're all putting in an extraordinary amount of work for a group of boisterous drunks."

Gavin's laugh was explosive. She loved it. She wanted to kiss him for it but she didn't.

"Well, there is a formal ball on the first day. This is when our father will present you as his daughter to the rest of the clan."

Wow. The clan. These were her people.

"I still haven't figured out the whole "I'm Scottish" thing yet...I love that I am an American but now there's this other half of me that I really know nothing about. Another culture to figure out how I fit into."

"Maybe you need to figure out how it fits into you?"

"Wow. He's deep."

"He is at that." Gavin smirked. "The majority of the people who will be attending are distant relatives. They'll be very excited to meet you."

"No pressure or anything." She rinsed out the last bit of grout on the sponge and thought about the enormity of

Gavin's last statement. "My entire life, I've been one-half of two people. I never really knew my mother's family. She was an only child and wasn't especially close to her parents. Now I'm the daughter of the Laird and I have a huge family to meet. I'm a bit overwhelmed." Rebecca caught Gavin's eye and her breath caught.

Gavin sensed the same heat between them and stood abruptly. He held out his hand to Rebecca very gallantly. "Wanna take a wee break?"

Rebecca was in desperate need of a massage and her arms were nearly falling off. "You have no idea. But I want to ask you a *wee* question first. You can't get mad." Rebecca rubbed the stiffness out of her neck.

"Well, when you start off like that…"

Rebecca flashed him her most innocent smile and he relented.

"Fine."

"Why'd you get mad when I agreed with James that you should become a Lord?"

He took a deep breath. "There's not an easy answer."

Rebecca smiled reassuringly. "Try me."

Gavin nodded and huffed out a quick laugh. "I don't feel as though I have any control over my life." He paused, she didn't interrupt. "Ever since I was young, decisions have been made for me that I've had no choice over." He picked absently at a piece of loose grout. "You will go to Eton, you will run this house when you are older, you will become a Lord. All of my life is wrapped up in this house, and I didn't choose this life."

"I'm the total opposite. I've not had any one tell me what to do my entire life. That's no picnic either."

"Seems there should be a happy medium."

"Agreed." Rebecca walked to the window and looked out at the vast beauty before her. "Although, most anyone I know would die to live like this."

He stepped up next to her and watched her for a moment before he followed suit and looked out the window. "I've tried to carve out a few places here that I have some say over... Things that are mine."

"The bees...the truffles?"

"Aye." He shook his head silently. "But in the end, those bits of independence still have to do with the estate. I just want to be inspired." He looked deep into Rebecca's eyes. "I thought you were that inspiration for me. You woke me up. And now..." He looked away.

"It's ok." She touched him briefly on his arm. "You woke me up too."

* * *

From the library window, which happened to overlook the glass ceiling of the atrium, Beatrice and James watched the closeness develop between Rebecca and Gavin.

"You're just gonna sweep this under the rug, then?"

"I thought I might."

"What are you afraid of?"

"Where do I begin?" James loved the boy more than life itself and the fact that he wasn't his blood didn't bother him. He'd gotten over the fact that Gavin's mother was unfaithful – never mind the arguments to the contrary from Braeden and Beatrice. But he was concerned that since he let this deception continue for so long, that Gavin wouldn't understand why he'd kept it from him.

Gavin liked to work the land but he never quite embraced his lineage. James knew that no matter how hard he tried to push Gavin toward a Lordship, a title, Gavin pushed back harder. It was almost like he knew he wasn't "of the blood."

"It's not like you've lied to him his whole life. It was more of an omission."

"I hope he sees it that way."

"So you're going to tell him?"

"I don't know."

The doorbell rang and Beatrice left James with one flippantly tossed comment "Sperm's overrated."

James knew this to be true. He had adopted Gavin as a child and loved him beyond measure. He named him in his will as the sole heir. There would be no debate that Gavin would inherit everything in the future but he just didn't want to go 'round shakin' the tree.

Chapter 25

Beatrice entered with a tray for tea and behind her was a very handsome man who was, very gallantly, helping her carry a second tray of finger sandwiches and fruit. "Rebecca. You have company."

"How can I have company? No one knows I'm here."

Beatrice set the tray down and patted her arm. "'Tis a small town, Darlin'. Everyone knows you're here."

The man attempted to clear up the confusion. "Ewan, from the pub, brought me 'round your cottage yesterday. There is quite an odor."

"Yeah. Gross, right?"

He nodded. "The couple from across the street told me where to find you."

And that wasn't weird or anything. "I've never even spoken to them. How the heck did they find out where I was?"

The man shrugged, and Gavin stood and offered his hand to the man. "And you are?"

He shook Gavin's hand but Beatrice answered for him before he could. "Inspector Sean O'Brian. He has a few questions for Rebecca."

Rebecca looked to Gavin for assistance. "I've only just arrived. I couldn't have broken the law this quickly."

The Inspector shook his head. "I heard you ran into some beehives? Is that correct?"

She shot a look of uncertainty toward Gavin. "Should I call Ned?"

Gavin took over the conversation again. "Inspector, perhaps if she knew what you needed from her…"

"Oh…yes, of course. I am investigating some recent bee thefts and my investigation led me here."

Rebecca immediately relaxed. "I just crashed into them, I didn't steal them."

A deep throaty growl from Biscuit preceded James into the atrium. Seeing the Inspector, James ushered the dog outside then extended his hand in welcome to the Inspector. "Well, hello there, son. I'm Lord McDermott."

"Inspector Sean O'Brian."

"Nothing serious I hope."

"Bees."

"Good. Good. Tea?"

Sean shook his head. "Nothing for me."

James was determined. "You must have tea."

Sean complied and helped himself. "Cheers."

Beatrice watched the oddly similar behavior between James and the Inspector with interest and after a moment, abruptly interrupted the banter. "Oh, right I forgot. Inspector, I'll just go see if Braeden is available."

Sean smiled warmly at Beatrice. "Thank you. I shouldn't be but a minute longer."

Rebecca took a sip of her tea. "When did you figure out the bees were stolen?"

The Inspector flipped open a notepad. "Several days ago."

"Before or after I hit them?"

"After." Sean laughed warmly. "Do you mind if I ask the questions?"

"Go for it."

"Please, tell me what happened."

"That's not a question." She couldn't resist.

Gavin raised an eyebrow giving her a slight smirk.

She shrugged. "I'm just *takin' a piss* as you all say."

Sean took it in stride and even laughed. "You are correct. Can you tell me what happened?"

"Well. I was driving, trying to stay on the right side of the road, which is really hard to do, by the way."

"We drive on the left side so I can see where you may have had trouble." Sean smirked.

She liked this guy. There was something really comforting and familiar about him.

"Fine." She acquiesced. "The *correct* side of the road. Those suckers are really narrow. You'd think someone would, at the very least, paint the center line yellow like they do in the States…" She looked around the room for support but received only blank looks. "How do you even know which roads are one way and which are two-way roads?"

Sean tapped his pencil on the notepad. "So the bees…"

"Right, I was changing the song on the radio and looking at the beautiful landscape and I almost hit Chewbacca…"

Sean stopped writing. "Excuse me?"

Gavin laughed, and Rebecca's heart did its usual flip. "She means a highland cow."

"Ah. Right." He jotted that note down although he didn't really know why. He doubted that the presence of a cow would get him any closer to finding the stolen bees. "Please continue."

"I had to swerve around the hairy beast and I ran off the road…into the hives."

"Ok…Do you remember what the hives looked like?"

"No. I wasn't really paying attention."

"Clearly."

"Hey. I was running for my life. There were a lot of bees."

"Color? Size? Amount?"

"Of bees?"

"Hives."

"Lots. I told you I wasn't really looking at them."

Gavin spoke up. "They were gray."

Sean stopped writing. "You know this how?"

"I was there. That's where we met. After she hit the bees."

"Do you remember anything else?"

"No."

At that moment, Beatrice entered. "Inspector, Braeden is ready for you."

"If I have any further questions, I know where to find you." He cracked the slightest smile and followed Beatrice out.

Beatrice tried to appear more casual than she felt. "Where did you say you were from?"

"Glasgow."

Beatrice nodded thoughtfully. "Born there were ya?"

"No. I was actually born here, at Newtonmore Hospital."

"Aye?"

"This area was one of my parents' favorite camping spots…I guess I arrived a bit earlier than they expected."

Beatrice shook her head in contemplation. "Camping… I've never understood why anyone would want to pretend to be homeless."

Chapter 26

The walk to the Apiary from the house took about five minutes and Sean was happy for the chance to stretch his legs. He could have questioned Braeden while they walked but he didn't have that many questions for him so he held them until they arrived at the apiary...And he didn't want to ruin this perfect moment of silence. He didn't get that many of them.

The McDermott Apiary was a very small operation compared to the other apiaries he investigated over the past few days. On initial examination, their business looked pretty straight forward: Bees, honey, a few sales.

Standing there in the beekeeper's hat, watching Braeden smoke the bees and cut into the golden comb, Sean thought for the first time in his life, that he could be happy doing something other than law enforcement. That revelation came as a shock to him because the thought of doing anything other than what he was doing never even crossed his mind until this past week, when he mistakenly arrested the Chief's niece for prostitution...

Sean knew he was a good cop. His father was a cop and his grandfather was one as well, so law enforcement was an easy fit. He never really considered a career in anything else. After he spent his requisite four years in the British Army as a sharpshooter, he immediately transitioned to the Police Training School.

Sean's parents died in a car accident when he was eighteen. Being an only child and having nothing to tie him down, Sean opted to enlist in the British Army. He had a great run of it and secured himself a powerful letter of recognition from his commander stating that he was, among other things, "An honest man with great heart and conviction." That heart and conviction and the fact that he was in great shape helped Officer Sean O'Brian to become Inspector Sean O'Brian in short order.

The biggest mistake of his career was two weeks ago. He was given a tip by a local source that there was a large prostitution ring being formed at the University. His source, Bitsie, a transvestite from Galloway, had never given him bad information in the past. Her information helped him close many cases over the years so Sean had no reason to question the validity by double-checking the information. He ordered a full-scale raid and as a result, ended up arresting seventeen young men and women for prostitution. One of them being Chief Inspector Hollister's niece.

She was *allegedly* there for a Halloween party along with several of her friends and swore up and down that she wasn't part of whatever had been going on there in the previous months.

No one knew for sure what really went down and all of the charges against her were eventually dropped but not before the news station played the arrest over and over again. The Chief was mortified, his niece was embarrassed, and Sean got a taste of their vengeance.

Chief Inspector Hollister was not a small man, and although he was in his late 60's, he was by no means out of shape. He towered over Sean by a good three inches- and Sean was nearly six feet.

The Chief dropped a large box of files on Sean's desk the next morning. "Here ya go, Inspector."

"What's this?"

"My gift to you for arresting my niece." The Chief grinned vengefully and shoved the box around so Sean could read the words BEE THEFTS- HIGHLANDS written on the front.

"She looked very convincing as a prostitute, sir." Sean stood and looked around the precinct at the thinly suppressed snickerers. "She…I had no way of knowing…I…" The room erupted in laughter.

"How do you suppose Sunday lunch at my sister's house is going to be next week?

"It'll be shite, I wager." Sean knew the question was rhetorical. He should have kept his mouth shut.

"Aye, most definitely. And, since I can't fire ye, you are heading to the Highlands. There was another theft."

"That bee case is a joke, Sir, and it's not under our jurisdiction."

The Chief smiled without joy. "Lucky for you a position just opened up in the Northern Constabulary. You've been re-assigned."

Sean was not about to back down. "There hasn't been a solid lead in over three years!"

The Chief's face was transitioning from pink to very dark red before Sean's eyes. "You'd better find one Inspector… Or you will be up there for a very long time. There was another theft yesterday."

"You can't be serious."

A sinister smile crossed the Chief's face. "Clear out your desk. You leave within the hour." As if to punctuate his resolve, the Chief slapped the daily newspaper onto the table in front of Sean. *Bee Thief Stings the Highlands* was the headline.

Everyone on the force knew of this case. It was a career breaker for anyone attached to it. According to this new article: Bees worth thousands of pounds had been reported stolen across Britain, with the most high-profile theft taking place two weeks ago.

Eleven hives, containing up to 500,000 bees, apparently destined for the Balmoral Royal Estate in Scotland were stolen. Sean knew the frequency of thefts had been increasing over the past several years and there were several fresh cases reported over the past few months, but there were never any good leads, and none of the stolen bees were ever found. Probably because none of the thefts were connected to each other. It was a dog of a case. A case used to punish and humiliate and now he had no choice but to try to solve it or be stuck in the Highlands forever.

After he had packed the last of his things, he headed toward the door. The eyes of the entire office were on his back. He turned and looked straight at the Chief Inspector. "I'll solve this case and return straight away. Best not to fill my desk just yet." And with that, he shut the door on the room, drowning out the latent burst of laughter.

He loaded everything into the car, stopped by his flat to grab the necessities, and reluctantly headed off to Inverness.

It wasn't as though he disliked the Highlands. It was beautiful to be sure, but everyone Sean knew lived in Glasgow. All of his friends were there. His life was there. He wasn't afraid of change- he had been through plenty of that in the past eighteen years, but he finally found a groove of sorts in Glasgow and he wasn't eager to leave. Especially not to be dragged down by this epically unsolvable case.

But now, here he was in the Highlands...

Braeden handed a section of the honeycomb to Sean who was immediately surprised at how excellent the honey tasted. "This is brilliant."

Braeden was clearly proud of the operation he and Gavin had going. "Indeed. In my opinion, the best honey comes from bees in the wild. Or bees who think they're wild, at any rate."

Sean licked the residual honey off his fingers and took out his notebook. "No doubt you've made a packet."

"We do alright,"

"Where did you get your bees?"

"Well, the wild ones were already here. Just there." He pointed to a beehive attached to the exterior edge of the cave that was dripping with honey. "That's why we chose this place to set up in the first place. The other bees and hives you see there on the ground; we acquired several years ago."

"Acquired from where?"

"I dunno. You'll have to ask Gavin that."

Sean stepped further into the depths of the cave. "What's back there?"

"Natural aquifer. It goes back quite aways."

"Mind if I have a wee poke around?"

The rain had started its deluge again and it didn't look like it would let up any time soon. Braeden pulled the hood of his rain jacket over his head and stepped out from the protection of the cave. "Not at all. Best hurry up though or come back in a couple days if it suits you. Looks like we're in for a bit more flooding."

Sean thought about it for a moment. "Yeah…Yeah I'll come back later."

* * *

Beatrice burst through the doors of the local hospital and made a b-line toward the break room.

Maggie smiled at her good friend. "Ah Beatrice, luv. What brings you here? You ill?"

"No I'm hale, dear. I have a wee favor."

"Aye. Anything."

"I need you to try to remember something."

Maggie shook her head slowly. "You know that's not somethin' I'm good at."

Beatrice knew her friend had had a rough time of it. Maggie had taken up the drink decades ago after her daughter, Fiona, passed and had been sober off and on through the years...*mostly off.* "I need you to remember the night Gavin was born."

"That was a long time ago, Bea. I don't even remember the night me own Fiona was born, God rest her." Maggie crossed herself then grew quiet.

"Aye, darlin', but try...Was there a second bairn born that same night?"

"I dunna know. My mind isn't as sharp as it used to be."

Beatrice patted her hand. "Just think on it. And get back to me if something comes to mind."

"Aye. I will. See ya at the Gatherin'?"

That was Maggie's not so subtle way of assuring herself that she was still invited to attend. Last year she had fallen so far off her wagon she had to be removed from the event because she wouldn't let anyone else near the chocolate fondue fountain and Ewan nearly lost a limb. "Aye Maggie. See ya at the Gatherin'. But be a dear and leave your wee sabre at home."

Maggie smirked sheepishly. "Aye."

Chapter 27

Gavin checked out his reflection in the mirror. He never minded dressing in full Savile Row bespoke. He knew it looked good on him and he liked to wear *finery* from time to time, but not today. There was far too much to do around the estate to get ready for the Gathering, and the last thing he wanted to do was to get on the train for the twelve-hour trek to London.

His decision of finally agreeing to the trip most certainly had to do with Rebecca and his need to have some time away from her to clear his head. But it was also because of her that he felt like he could, in good conscience, leave with just days to get the estate ready. She was a quick and very skilled craftswoman, and they had achieved more over the past several days together than he ever thought was possible.

They were even able to take a substantial amount of the burden off of Braeden who, since his actual title at the estate was *the Gillie*, was finally able to prepare for the annual MacNab Challenge that James insisted they have every year. And every year, they still had more and more issues which needed repair at the crumbling estate. He hoped that his agreeing to accept this new title would soften his father to the prospect of discussing the National Trust -and he most certainly would be a Lord by the end of the day.

The Appointments Committee had already recommended him as non-party-political life peer and this meeting with Lord Dillinger was merely a formality. Since agreeing to the peerage, his father had seen to it that his nomination was announced and this meeting was simply to introduce Gavin to the other Lords of the House. He still didn't know why it was so important to his father that he be a Lord in his own right, but his father's persistence (aided by Rebecca's sudden appearance) finally won out, and Gavin gave in.

"Best get on with it, mate." His reflection scowled back at him as he finished adjusting his tie.

* * *

Gavin didn't see his cab in the driveway when he exited the estate, so to kill some time, he took a brisk walk to the lake to check on the progress of the rock wall and gazebo. He found Rebecca, standing at the edge of the lake, her arms hugging her light jacket around her. She turned upon hearing him approach. The look in her bright eyes when she saw him nearly melted his heart, and he internally chastised himself for not waiting for the cab inside like most people.

Rebecca was dumbstruck. Gavin was beautiful…"Wow. You look really nice." At least she managed to keep the compliment neutral. Truth was, he looked really, really, really, extraordinarily hot. His broad shoulders and tapered waist were things of perfection, and her mind couldn't help drifting to the day they spent together at the ruins and the beautiful moment they had with each other after they got back to her place. She couldn't take her eyes off him. She gripped her jacket tighter to stop herself from reaching out and touching him. "Like, really, really nice."

Gavin laughed warmly. "Thank you. I'm off to the big smoke."

"I have no idea what that is."

"London. Big city. Lots of smoke."

"Sounds ominous."

"Truly."

"So next time I see you, you will be a Lord?"

"Tomorrow night."

Rebecca's eyes lit up.

"What does that look mean?"

"Nothing." She was beyond ecstatic to hear she would only have to endure a couple more days of silence…She hoped. "It's just that I'm excited to be in the presence of two Lairds." She could see that he wasn't actually buying her explanation but that couldn't be helped. She wanted to tell him so badly but that bomb needed to come from James.

Gavin sensed her mood shift, and he assumed she wanted to talk about their paternity. They would, at some point, have to talk about it but neither one of them wanted to start that conversation.

And now was definitely not that time.

He'd go to London, become a Lord and hopefully, things would be more bearable upon his return tomorrow night.

He wasn't at all happy about the fact that he would be arriving back at the estate only hours before all of the guests arrived but it couldn't be helped. At least the house wouldn't fall down around everyone's heads while they were enjoying the festivities- thanks to Rebecca.

The taxi arrived, and Gavin climbed into the back. "Well, wish me luck."

Rebecca's countenance suddenly dropped. "Do you need it? I mean…Could something go wrong?"

Again, Gavin sensed that Rebecca was alluding to something but didn't come out and say it.

"Not likely. My father took care of everything so I just need to show up."

Rebecca visibly relaxed. "That's good."

It didn't take a genius to figure out that whatever she was concerned about had something to do with him and this whole, *becoming a Lord*, business. "Well, I best be going. Don't want to be late." He'd have to add that to the list of things to ask her about when he returned home.

Rebecca watched the cab head down the long drive and drifted off into another more manageable realm.

She wasn't certain how long she was blacked out for but when she awoke, she was in a strange bed, in a strange room and a strange woman was sleeping in a chair next to her. When the woman heard her ask where she was, the woman screamed with joy and ran out of the room. Moments later, her father, the King entered, tears streaking down his face.

He looked fragile and weak, and Abigail was so thankful Ciro had agreed to bring her to him. She missed Ciro desperately though. She wondered at the emptiness in her heart that she had never felt before.

"Oh my daughter. I thought you dead."

"I am well, as you see."

They wept and hugged and Abigail shared her story about Ciro. The King was thankful to the dragon as the Viking king had heard of Abigail's beauty and demanded to have her as his wife. She was assumed dead and that was that.

In the shadows, a dark figure lurked and listened to the story of the brave, sweet dragon. Balthazar was unaware Ciro had found himself a human. He was taken aback at the discovery that Ciro was getting more cunning.

"Rebecca?"

She jumped and turned around to find Patrick staring at her, grinning broadly. "You were somewhere else. I called you at least three times."

"What are you doing here?"

"I told you I would pop by."

"I asked you to call first."

Patrick shrugged and threw her a cocky smirk.

"When did you get here? I didn't see you drive up."

"Got here bright and early this morning. Braeden needed help on the roof."

Rebecca narrowed her gaze, then she stepped toward the house without comment.

Patrick followed her in silence for a few paces then raced around to face her. "Listen. About me and Gavin. I was an arse. I know that. I will always be an arse where Gavin is concerned, but I am sorry I used you to get to him."

She tried to pass him but he caught her arm and stopped her from walking away. "You don't have to forgive me." He shrugged. "I'm really beyond forgiveness anyway." He shook his head solemnly. "Listen, I need some help picking up some things for the Gathering, and Braeden said you were the only one he could spare."

She stared at him for a long minute and took a deep breath in resolution. "I'm gonna check with Braeden first. As long as he doesn't need me here, I'll help you out." She wouldn't be caught dead with Patrick otherwise. She shook her arm free and headed toward the front door tossing the next comment over her shoulder. "And…I agree; you are an ass. Also, you need to keep your hands to yourself."

"I can do that." Patrick smirked and then his eyes roamed her body.

She sensed him looking at her and rounded on him. "And your eyes…Wanker."

Patrick laughed to himself. He would be lying if he said he wasn't interested in her, but he wasn't entirely sure he wanted to put in the effort he knew it would take to woo her. Especially now that she was Gavin's sister. He'd never be out of Gavin's shadow, and that was not a place he liked to be.

Chapter 28

The ride to Inverness was a wet one, but for a brief moment, the rain stopped, and the sky cleared and Rebecca saw what was probably the most magnificent sight in the entire country. Maybe the entire world.

The fog was visibly thick after the rain and looked like it was shrouding a structure of some sort. As Patrick made a turn toward Drumnadrochit the structure -the Urquhart Castle she later discovered- appeared out of the fog like a spectre. As the sun began to shine, the fog rose to reveal a spectacular stone structure rising above Loch Ness. The lake turned the most magnificent shade of blue contrasting with the verdant green hills where the castle's keep stood sentry. Rebecca was unable to look away as she pictured Abigail running from Balthazar who held her captive in this very place:

Abigail thought her lungs would burst if she continued running at this pace. She didn't know how much longer her bare feet could stand the rocky ground beneath her but she knew she had to continue.

The orange mist seemed to cling to every fiber of her clothing and pull her back toward her pursuers. She kicked and fought and barely managed to escape its grip only to be hit with tiny darts across her back. Her only hope was to make it into the dense, dark forest. She needed to find a place to hide.

Another wave of painful, fiery darts seared her skin and she lunged toward a large boulder just outside of the forest. She screamed in agony and fell into the mist as a pair of large hands enveloped her and covered her mouth.

"Don't scream." He gestured to the soldiers searching nearby.

Abigail turned to see the kindest green eyes staring back at her. She was so taken with the man that she wasn't even overly concerned that he was holding his hand over her mouth and nodded her willingness to obey his request.

One of the soldiers turned back directly in front of them and Abigail held her breath, afraid that they would hear her heart pounding just feet away. "I lost her."

"Where did you see her last?"

"At the edge of the forest."

The men hurried their way toward the forest's edge and the hand over her mouth was removed. "I am the man who has waited his entire life to save you, dear Abigail. Although, it could be said that you saved me first"

Abigail continued to gaze directly into the eyes of her savior, and her thanks caught in her throat. He looked very familiar. Almost like…CIRO! She nearly died with shock.

They caught up with the rain a few miles past the castle and soon, she saw signs for Inverness as Patrick drove her past the tip of the long Loch Ness. "Thought you'd like to see a bit more of the land since you were so taken by that wee glimpse of the castle. We'll climb the stairs of the North Tower. It used to be a county prison back in the day."

"A tower? I thought we were picking up supplies."

He saw her mistrust. "I thought we'd have a wee climb to stretch our legs and have a drink before we do the heavy lifting."

"It's a wonder you get anything done."

"In my opinion, this is the best view in the Highlands." From the parking lot, the structure was a little pinkish in color. It was actually quite beautiful, but she would reserve her opinion as to whether she agreed it was the best view, until after she had a look.

The irony of the situation struck her: Patrick the *wide-boy* actually chose to voluntarily enter a prison -well former county prison- and he thought that this was the best view in the Highlands. Rebecca nearly laughed out loud.

They walked through the doors of the public building, and with a nod to the security guard, Patrick walked her through a door that was designated "Employees Only."

"Not open to the public yet. But I know some people."

"I bet you do."

The door led to a steep, wooden staircase of four stories but once they exited onto the roof, the view from the top was impressive. Although Rebecca didn't prefer this to the view from the ruins- not by a longshot, the view was quite beautiful. She wouldn't go so far as to say it was the *best view in the Highlands* as touted to her by her host but as Patrick pointed out, "You can see the River Ness from here and the Great Glen."

"It is beautiful."

Patrick smiled down at her. "I come up here to think sometimes." His eyes roamed over the city and the view beyond. "I used to watch the cars passing and wonder who was in them and how they got their money. Who they were shaggin'. You know."

Rebecca wasn't quite sure how to respond to that.

His eyes turned serious. "I don't owe anybody anything."

She wasn't quite sure how to respond to that either but she gave it a stab. "I guess that's a good position to be in."

"Aye. It is." He sighed deeply.

She felt that she was being given a small glimpse into the real Patrick, if only for a moment. Although his comment was a little cryptic if not superficial, she got the impression that it was important to him that he be independent…free of constraint. She couldn't fault him for that.

She still didn't want to spend any more time with him than she needed to and was eager to return to the estate.

He turned to face her. "Drinks."

And they were back in the van.

*　*　*

Rebecca was only five-foot-six but she had to stoop down to enter through the door of the Pinfield Inn and Pub. She was in awe that the country had buildings like this that were still standing after hundreds of years. The ceiling was listing to the right and the thick, black beams supporting the white plaster walls were straining to keep the entire building from falling over. If this building were in the U.S., it would probably have been condemned centuries ago (or turned into a museum).

Inside, the pub was warm and dry despite the deluge of rain just outside the thick plaster and wood walls. A fire burned in the large fireplace, which was built into one of the walls. Patrick clearly felt at home. He walked directly to a booth, and immediately relaxed into the cushions.

He seemed to know everyone. He reciprocated the smiles and nods from the other patrons as they passed and he accepted several handshakes and pats on the back from others. Within the span of a few minutes, several beers and a couple of whiskies had been set in front of them; courtesy of this person or that person. Patrick was certainly *the man*. Rebecca smiled at the thought. He was not someone who would be apt to settle down with the 2.5 kids, dog and picket fence. He was very similar to Cameron that way. Rebecca was so thankful she could look outside the *show* and get a glimpse of the man.

A beautiful Miss America-looking blonde slid up on Patrick's other side and whispered in…or chewed on Patrick's ear. Rebecca couldn't tell which but after she removed herself from the bench Rebecca noticed that Miss America left a nice red lipstick mark on his cheek. Yep. She was glad she was on the outside.

"You're very popular, aren't you?'

Patrick shrugged with feigned humility. "Ach. If you can get somebody something for cheap they'll always buy you a drink. And they'll still feel like they owe ya."

"You must be very good at your job."

He nodded and pushed one of the whiskies toward her. She thanked him but only sipped at it since the last thing she'd eaten was breakfast, and they hadn't yet ordered. She didn't want to relive her recent boxed-wine or Benadryl incidents.

He tossed back the shot and chased it with half of a beer.

Rebecca just watched him thinking of a clever way to separate him from his van keys if he were to get drunk.

Patrick's phone rang and he made no apologies in answering it. "Right…Sure…Give me an hour." He turned to her "We should go. I've got a bit of business tonight."

"Tonight?"

"'Tis the best time to find things that fall off the back of a lorry."

"Ah…got it…Wide boy."

"I prefer 'Acquisitions and Delivery.'"

The server smiled sweetly at Patrick as they stood to leave. "Have ya found that flat screen for me mum yet?"

Before Patrick could respond, Rebecca locked eyes with the server. "I've got one at my place you can have." Rebecca certainly didn't want to be on the *owing end* of this *friendship*.

He nodded between her and the server. "Well it's settled then. I'll just go get it now." He saw the look of confusion cross Rebecca's face and answered before she could get the words out. "You don't live there anymore. Would have been a shame to waste a perfectly good telly." He smirked like the Cheshire Cat.

"I can't fault your logic. Need help carrying that in?" She teased.

"No!…No I'll take care of it." Patrick was a bit too emphatic with his refusal.

Rebecca wasn't expecting that kind of response to what she thought was an obviously sarcastic offer of assistance. Now she suspected that he was hiding something from her, which only made her curious to see what was in the back of his van. She expected to find the fondue pot along with the TV, but was secretly afraid that he had pilfered the furniture from her rental. Rebecca shrugged nonchalantly, covering her suspicion. "Ok. I'll just wait here then."

He relaxed and she waited a few moments before she poked her head out the side door to see if the coast was clear before sneaking around to where he had parked the van. But to her surprise, the van was now conveniently parked in front the side door and totally open to her view. There wasn't much of anything in the van besides the TV but what Rebecca did see scared her to death.

There were beehives tied to the back wall. They were gray and looked very much like the ones Rebecca slammed into upon her arrival. Her vision blurred and she began shaking. She ran to the bathroom and tried to stop hyperventilating. She had never had a panic attack before but growing up, she had seen patients at the hospital having them and the only thing they could do about them before they were sedated was to take deep breaths or pass out. She opted for the first choice and tried to take deep breaths.

Once she had finally calmed down, questions began to surface. First and foremost: How was she going to get into that van for the ride home now that she knew what was waiting for her? She was terrified. There was only a little slider window separating her from the bees and that freaked her the heck out.

Rebecca considered calling a taxi or taking the train home, but Patrick was smart enough to pick up on her change of behavior, and he would certainly deduce that Rebecca knew something. She was pretty sure he wasn't a killer, but when faced with the prospect of freedom or jail, Rebecca didn't really know what he would be capable of. And Rebecca was definitely going to call that Inspector when she got home…IF she got home. She started to hyperventilate again.

A few minutes later, she walked out of the bathroom and was happy to see that the whiskey hadn't been cleared from the table yet. Rebecca downed her shot for courage and Patrick's for good measure, and headed out the front door to face her imminent demise: If Patrick didn't kill her, the fear of those bees surely would.

Chapter 29

Patrick thought Rebecca was acting strangely when she hopped into his van about an hour ago and after seeing the text messages on her phone, he thought he knew why.

She had fallen asleep nearly the minute she returned to the van, and when Patrick stopped at their first location he tried to wake her so she could help him load the van, but she slept like the dead. So much for her help.

He was very glad that she was so compliant earlier when she offered to help unload the TV but he declined it. He had secreted some beehives behind the TV and didn't want her to see them in there. He didn't think she'd mind sitting this one out, and clearly she hadn't, because while she waited, she finished every bit of alcohol left on the table. And now, much to Patrick's annoyance, her phone kept buzzing with text messages while she slept through the noise.

Patrick, not being one to invade another's privacy, picked up her phone and scrolled through several days of messages between her and someone called Lacy.

I'm not related to him!
What?!! Tell me more!
I overheard James (my dad) talking with Beatrice about it.
I know James is your dad…aaaaand?
And she was trying to get James to tell Gavin.
Did you tell Gavin?
No….

WTF!! TELL HIM!!!

I can't. Something about the House of Lords not finding out or something.

Why do they care?

Not totally sure.

TELL HIM OR I WILL!!

You don't have his number…nice try though. I can't tell him. If he knew, I actually think somehow that would prevent him from becoming a Lord.

You don't do anything normal.

Tell me about it.

The rest of the messages weren't of much use to Patrick, but they were entertaining.

Rebecca shifted in her seat and Patrick quickly soft-booted her message program and tossed the phone on the floor at her feet before she came fully awake. He had two choices… He could either keep silent or tell Gavin about his paternity himself. Obviously, the second option would have the most gratification for him.

He was aware that Gavin would most likely end up with Rebecca either way, and there was nothing he could do about that at this point. But he could try to prevent Gavin from becoming a Lord. He knew that Gavin's sense of morality would prevent him from accepting the peerage if he knew he didn't deserve one, and as this was the final meeting, it was now or never. Just one more thing to shove in Gavin's face. Patrick was thrilled that "Mr. High and Mighty" was just a regular bloke like he was. He couldn't wait to rub that fact in. Gavin wasn't really a part of the aristocracy. Patrick laughed to himself at the revelation that Gavin was just like him, a nobody of inconsequential birth. They were truly equals, and Patrick was so very happy that he was the one who would break that news to him.

Patrick pulled to a stop on the side of the road and texted Gavin immediately.

Hey mate.
What?
Just want to see if you are a Lord yet.
Why do you care?
I rather like having one in my pocket.
…
You still there?
Yes.
Are you?
Not yet. Going in now. Why?
Isn't Rebecca lovely when she sleeps?
You're a bastard. I'm blocking you from my phone.

Patrick knew he shouldn't have pushed Gavin that far but it was so tempting trying to get a reaction out of him.

Sorry Wait!! I have something to tell you.
…
You still there?
What?

Patrick knew that Gavin had seen his final message. It said "read." Talk about cutting it close. He knew he was being an arse, but he just couldn't help but try to get the upper hand where Gavin was concerned.

* * *

Gavin was pissed. He knew Patrick was just trying to get a rise out of him for the hundredth time and he wished he could take everything in stride but he wasn't built that way. How the hell did he know what Rebecca looked like when she slept?

He paced back and forth in front of the House and considered hopping on the train now so he could punch Patrick in the face just that much sooner. He didn't know why he continued to allow himself to be goaded by him.

Apparently, he had some news. Whatever it was wouldn't be good but he couldn't help himself. He texted him back...

"Sir?" A smartly dressed young man was beckoning Gavin to follow him. "This way, please."

Gavin checked his phone for the return message and saw that Patrick was still typing.

"Phones off in the House, Sir."

"Of course." Gavin switched off his phone and followed the man inside. This was it. He'd sign the blasted papers in front of Lord Dillinger and be sworn in in a matter of moments.

An hour later, Gavin was finally finished shaking hands with the hundreds of men present and was cornered on his way out by the very persistent, Lord Dillinger. "Are you certain you can't join us for a drink, Lord McDermott?"

"My apologies, Lord...It's after 8 pm already and I've got to get home by tomorrow afternoon. The Gathering. You know."

"Yes. That I do. I had such a grand time last year. Nearly got the McNab. Damned salmon."

Gavin nodded with understanding. "Well, you're always welcome."

"Thank you. I'll leave you to it."

Gavin hailed a taxi to the station and promptly caught the train back to Inverness where, twelve hours later, he would take another taxi to Newtonmore.

He wasn't very successful in trying to forget Rebecca on his trip down, of course he'd slept for most of it, but he would have to conquer this on the long ride home. She was his sister for God's sake!

He relaxed in his seat and turned on his phone and saw the missed message from Patrick.

It was a good thing he was sitting down.

Listen, Rebecca overheard your father and Beatrice talking about the fact that you weren't actually his son. He knew you wouldn't go through with the peerage if you knew, but I didn't think that was fair so I thought I'd tell you before you made a fool of yourself.

Gavin was in complete shock. His whole life was just flipped over by the one man he could count on to always screw things up for him. Why was it that Patrick always seemed to be in the middle of the chaos in his life?

He was simultaneously ecstatic and pissed. His initial reaction was that Patrick was taking a piss but as much as he disliked Patrick at times, Patrick wasn't one to fabricate the truth.

Part of his irritation stemmed from the fact that apparently, Rebecca told Patrick about the origin of his birth but somehow neglected to let him in on the secret. Gavin gave her the benefit of the doubt, hoping that she found out about it after he had already gone to London. On the other hand, He wasn't related to Rebecca...And for that, he was eternally grateful.

And then there was the matter of Beatrice...If she knew, Braeden knew and if Braeden knew certainly, Ned also knew. What possessed them to keep the secret for so long? When did they find out? And how did they know he wasn't related?

He continued to vacillate back and forth through emotions spanning between elation and horror and finally landed on unbelief. How the hell could his dad…well, James, lie to him his entire life?

Gavin started to speed dial James and then stopped short. He had no idea what he would even say to him. He didn't want to admit that Patrick had gotten to him but most importantly, he needed to look James in the eye when he confronted him about the situation. Patrick wasn't the most trustworthy of persons.

He was glad for the additional time he had left on his ride home so he could attempt to calm down before speaking with James.

Questions tumbled out of his brain.

Was he adopted? Did his mother cheat on James? Who was his real father? What on earth was he going to do with the title he didn't even deserve? He couldn't just give it back. As pissed off as he was about Patrick's interference, he would have liked to have known the facts of his heritage before waltzing in to the House of Lords and accepting the peerage. As much as he despised Patrick right now, it seemed that he was the only one interested in telling him the truth.

Chapter 30

By the time Patrick finally dropped Rebecca off at the estate, she was hungry and had a huge crick in her neck from falling asleep in the van. But she was alive and stinger-free so that in itself was a huge victory. She headed straight for the kitchen hoping to catch someone in act of cooking. She found Beatrice and James.

Beatrice was already ladling stew into some bowls. "Come on in, Luv. Would you care for some dinner?"

"If it's no trouble." It seemed that from the time she arrived in Scotland she was either soaked to the bone or really hungry...or both. Beatrice handed her a large helping of stew along with a thick slice of homemade bread, slathered with butter. "This looks amazing!"

Rebecca caught James smiling oddly at her. "Have you anything to wear to the Gathering?"

"I don't know. What's the dress code?"

"Most days it's very casual but the first night, you will need a gown. Do you have a formal gown?"

"No." Rebecca laughed at the thought of her state of mind when she first left the States, and nearly choked on her stew. "The thought of packing a nice dress didn't even occur to me, but I did manage to fill my suitcase with a plethora of shorts and tank tops." She smiled sheepishly "I had a bit of a hangover."

James laughed heartily. "Well, you and I must go shopping for a gown tomorrow...and perhaps a proper Scottish pullover or two. Let's say 10 am."

Rebecca was stunned. "You want to take me shopping?"

James nodded. "Of course I would. You're my daughter. It's time we get on with getting to know each other."

* * *

Rebecca's life had changed so dramatically between the time she boarded that plane until now. She never imagined she would know her father, let alone shop for dresses with him but here she was, and by the time they had finished shopping, she felt more grounded somehow and was truly content for the first time in a long time.

As uncomfortable as it sounded to her when James first suggested they go shopping, she was surprised to find that there was no awkwardness between them, and she was having a wonderful time spending the day with *her dad.*

She had nearly lost hope that she would find the right dress until she found a beautiful blue-plaid Alexander McQueen gown that was hidden behind some fluffy taffeta atrocity. "This one! I love this one."

The look on James's face when he saw the dress was an odd one and she wasn't sure what was going through his head as he looked between her and the gown. His eyes were wide and the pride radiating from them took Rebecca's breath away. "Do you know what that fabric is, Rebecca?"

"No." She shook her head. "Should I?"

"If I didn't believe you were my daughter before, I certainly believe it now." He smoothed his hand down the edge of the garment. "Those are the McDermott colors. That is the McDermott plaid."

Rebecca could feel tears welling up in her eyes as she stared at the dress. There were no words available to Rebecca at that moment. She glanced at James and checked the size of the gown. She nodded and walked up to the counter to pay without even trying it on.

"Aren't you going to try it on?" James asked.

"No," she said. "It's my size, it's our colors and it will fit." She smiled, feeling very triumphant. It was at that moment that her stomach decided to growl very loudly.

James laughed warmly. "Lunch?" He stated more than asked. "I know a nice pub."

James promptly paid for the dress before Rebecca could, and they dropped the dress and *sweaters* off at the car on the way to lunch.

Rebecca was eager to get to know her father better. She knew he was in the military but beyond that, she really didn't know much else about him. "Did you go to Eton as well as Gavin?"

James took a long pull of his tea. "For a while I had gone to Eton, but my grades didn't hold up, and I was dismissed. I matriculated from Rugby instead."

"Rugby? Like the game?"

"Yes, that is where the game started."

Rebecca nodded. "So that's pretty cool though." She caught his look. "But you didn't think it was the best school, so you made sure Gavin went to Eton?"

"Yes. At the time, Gavin had squared his young shoulders and stated rather forcefully, 'If you expect me to run this place when I am a man, then I should stay here and learn to manage it from you.' I know Gavin wasn't particularly fond of the rigor or the fact that he had to leave a perfectly good home and bedroom of his own at the age of thirteen, to move into a house of 50 boys for five years but I felt- and I still feel- that every man of importance in this country has a degree from Eton."

Rebecca laid her hand on her father's and smiled sweetly up at him. "Not every man of importance."

James nodded slowly and allowed a proud smile to grace his lips.

After their nice pub lunch, Rebecca announced that she had a few errands to run of the "personal nature" and not knowing anything about what that would entail for a young woman, James said he would leave her to it and would send a car back to retrieve her in an hour.

James was very much taken aback when Rebecca threw her arms around him and hugged him. "Thank you, James... uh...Dad." She pulled away and pecked him on the cheek. "I had an amazing day."

His eyes began to sting with tears and he cleared his throat in an attempt to squelch them. He thought it wouldn't do if his heart burst just then, so he forced himself to speak. "I had a lovely day as well, dear." He squeezed her hand and climbed into the back of the car. "See you at home."

Home. Rebecca wiped away an errant tear that managed to escape as she watched the car head away. Reality definitely trumped fantasy- at least where her father was concerned.

Chapter 31

While she stood outside the police station, she took a minute to think about what she was about to do. She had never turned anyone in before, and as much as she was annoyed with Patrick, she didn't want to hurt him. But she was fairly certain the bees in his van were the very same bees she ran into, and the same bees the Inspector was looking for. Besides, every single person in Newtonmore and the surrounding areas could probably vouch for his ability to find things that *fell off the back of a truck* so she figured it was fairly likely that this wasn't the first time his name was spoken of at the station.

Rebecca took a deep breath and ran *literally* into Sean as he was on his way out. They ended the collision in an awkward hug.

"Rebecca. It is a pleasure to see you again."

"I'm so glad I *ran into you*." She laughed. "I was just on my way to find you, actually."

"How can I help?"

"Well, I don't know if you can help me but I think I may be able to help you." She smirked.

Intrigued, Sean directed her toward an unused interrogation room where they could chat without being disturbed. "Really? Well, don't leave me in suspense." They sat across the steel table from each other and Sean leaned back in his chair with a confident and relaxed air.

There was something Rebecca liked very much about the Inspector. He really put her at ease and as much as she wanted to get the conversation over with, she really liked to talk to him. "I think I found your bees."

Sean's eyes widened in surprise. "Really? Where? How certain are you?"

Rebecca chuckled at his exuberance. "Well, to be honest, I'm not certain the bees I saw were the same bees you're looking for but they sure looked a lot like the ones I ran into."

"It would be good news if they were. Where did you find them?"

"In the back of Patrick Farrell's van."

"How sure are you?"

"I'd say ninety-five percent."

"That's a pretty good certainty."

"Yeah. I had a really visceral reaction to them when I saw them. Like PTSD or something."

"What color were they?"

"Gray and they had some red paint on them…probably from my car."

"Number?"

"Of bees? I didn't see any. Thank God!"

"Hives."

"Oh." Rebecca smiled. "This conversation is beginning to sound vaguely familiar."

"At least you're letting me ask the questions this time."

"Yes. I do seem to be." Rebecca smirked and then answered his previous question "I don't really know. Maybe five."

Sean was quiet for a moment. There should be at least ten hives, so he wasn't certain they were the same ones. He needed to get a look in the back of that van.

Rebecca broke him out of his rumination. "Are you going to the Gathering?"

Sean shook his head. "I wasn't invited. Why?"

"Patrick said he'd be there tonight. Consider yourself invited."

"Are you certain?"

"Well, I'm certain that he told me he'd be there." She shrugged. "He asked if I'd dance with him, but it's Patrick so, I couldn't tell you if he were serious or not."

Sean sat quietly in thought for a moment. "Thank you. I don't think I ever would have taken a look in his direction if you hadn't brought him up."

"No problem." Rebecca checked the time on her phone and stood. "Also, I'd rather you not mention where this tip came from. I'm still pretty new to this area, and I know there are a lot of people who benefit from Patrick's...uh... "services" and I know my family loves him...well, maybe not Gavin."

"Not a word."

Rebecca stood to leave and gave Sean the cheek-kiss-hug thing before she left the small room. "Oh! You need to dress kind of nice tonight."

"Will do. Thank you again for the invite."

* * *

After Rebecca left, Sean began looking into Patrick's past. He discovered Patrick had been arrested several times, but somehow, he always seemed to leave with a clean record. He had enough probable cause to get a warrant to search the back of his van, and Sean prayed that Patrick hadn't removed the bees since yesterday.

This was the first real lead this case had had in over three years.

Over the past weeks he came to love the Highlands- and the people- and could actually see himself staying here indefinitely. Although, this case wasn't nagging him to finish like it was before, he did want to wrap it up for the sake of accomplishing something, but he wasn't as eager to get back to his previous life in Glasgow.

As Sean leaned over a desk covered with photos from the various crime scenes over the past three years, his tall, gangly assistant, Officer Reid entered waving a large evidence folder above his head. "I have the photos you requested from the American's accident, Sir."

"It's about bloody time. I asked for them over a week ago."

"Aye. Budget cuts."

Sean laid the new evidence on the table and after perusing it for a few moments, he singled out one of the photos from Rebecca's accident and placed it next to another photo from a previous incident. He circled a set of tire tracks in each photo.

"Do these look like the same tracks to you?"

Officer Reid leaned over Sean's shoulder to take a closer look. "Aye. They do. Do you think this could be something?"

Sean shrugged. "One can only hope." Sean sat back and shook his head in disbelief. "I thought it would take me at least three years to get a lead on this case." The pace was much slower than in Glasgow. He had time to think and, although he was still working on an impossible case, until now, he was more content here than he had ever been in the Lowlands.

"Well, I won't say that I'd be sorry to have this case put to rest, but I would be sorry to have you leave us. We've all grown rather fond of you here."

"I'm rather fond of you all as well."

Chapter 32

Gavin needed to speak with his father but he wanted to know the scope of his deception first so he could enter into the battle prepared. If James taught him anything, it was to enter every battle with as much information as you could in order to best defeat your enemy. This way of thinking helped Gavin come out on top in many a business dealing. Not that his father was his enemy, but Gavin wanted to be prepared for everything that could come up – or at least have the assurance from a trusted family friend that what Patrick said was in fact, the truth.

Gavin burst through the doors of the Fox and Hen and was greeted by a full house of very well-dressed regulars getting a start on the festivities. They would all be well into their cups by the time they arrived at the estate for the Gathering tonight.

"Anyone see Ned?" Gavin yelled over the cacophony.

Evelyn and Archie were seated at one of the tables near the door and Evelyn tapped Gavin on the arm to get his attention. "He just stepped out. I think he said he was headed to Boots."

"Thanks, Evelyn…Archie. See you tonight?"

"Aye. That you will."

Gavin headed out the door and caught Ned just as he was exiting the drug store. "Ned. Got a minute?"

"Aye. Is this a professional minute or a friendly minute?"

"A little of both, I'd wager." Gavin sat on a nearby bench. "I'd best jump right in."

Ned sat curiously beside Gavin. "Aye."

"Am I or am I not James' son."

Ned smiled. He answered slowly, wanting to convey as much as he could without revealing too much. Being careful not to break the client-lawyer privilege he had with James. "You are his son…"

Gavin picked up on his facial language and inflection. "So what you're saying is, I am his son, but not his son."

"If that's what you think." Ned gave him a knowing smile.

"So by your reasoning, I am James' son but not necessarily Rebecca's brother."

Ned took a breath and contemplated his next statement. "You look nothing like her."

Gavin's smile could light up a room. He stood and smacked Ned genially on the arm as he headed out the door. "That is very true, Ned. Very true, indeed."

* * *

Gavin asked the taxi driver to drop him on the other side of the river as he still needed a moment to cool his heels before speaking with James. A dunk in the river and walk back to the house would be a start.

He removed his boots, vest and jacket, phone, wallet and keys and was tempted to jump in with the rest of his clothes on but decided against it. Instead, he removed all but his boxer shorts then waded into the river.

After a brief dip he was ready to head back to the estate and considered putting his pants on over his wet boxers but changed his mind. Since it was a half mile back to the house, he decided against making the trek in just his underwear. He backtracked to the barn and grabbed a clean horse blanket from the tack room and "kilted" it around his waist, securing it with his belt. He smiled at the thought of Rebecca and her general lack of clothing when they first met. Well, the first several times they were together if he was being honest.

She was beautiful. Even as swollen as she was and covered in green goop and pink lotion, he had fallen in love with her and he was even more anxious to see her now that they both knew the truth. He couldn't wait to speak with her, but he didn't know if they'd get the chance to be alone over the next few days.

He pulled his boots on and thought to himself that he looked very much like a Highland Warrior as he strode across the vast empty grounds of the estate. They wouldn't be empty for long. Within hours, the estate would be brimming with clansmen and women all dressed up for the formal event of the evening.

He passed by one of the very large tents and he heard a scuffling noise within, so he entered to see if he could help the workers with any last-minute tasks, but instead ran headlong into Rebecca, knocking her to the ground and nearly falling on top of her.

"Rebecca." He forced himself to stand up *he rather enjoyed the closeness* and helped her to her feet. He couldn't stop his hand from brushing a stray lock of hair from her beautiful face.

Rebecca nearly passed out at the sight of the Highland Warrior standing before her. It took her a minute to realize it was Gavin, and when she did, she couldn't stop herself from staring. He was shirtless after all.

Gavin couldn't take his eyes off of her either. Especially when he saw her lips curl into a seductive smile as her eyes roamed over his body. "Is this what they do to you after you become a Lord?" She joked.

Gavin laughed heartily.

"Are you a Lord?"

"Aye." He stood still and watched her look him up and down.

He was delicious. "Who knew a man could look so tasty in a skirt?"

"It's a kilt. As you know." Gavin couldn't stop himself from crushing his lips to hers.

Through his kisses, Gavin notified Rebecca that he knew they weren't related.

"I figured," she said and pressed her body into his warmth. She tangled her fingers in his hair, pulling his kiss deeper.

They heard a man clearing his voice behind Gavin and pulled out of the kiss, but Gavin kept his arm firmly around Rebecca's waist, unwilling to let her go.

Ned laughed. "You made quick work of it."

Gavin smiled his half-smile, and it took all of Rebecca's strength not to pull him back into her arms. "Aye."

Ned gave Gavin a firm pat on his shoulder. "It nearly did me in trying to figure out a way to tell you without break-ing the client-lawyer privilege I have with your father." He laughed and walked toward the house. "Best be getting inside. I want to sample the food before everyone else gets to it."

When Ned was out of earshot, Gavin turned toward Rebecca and took her hands. "How long have you known?"

Rebecca shrugged sheepishly. "The first night I was here. I overheard James and Beatrice talking in the kitchen. It was nearly impossible for me not to tell you."

"And you didn't think I had a right to know?"

"Of course I did. I just knew that James thought it was an important secret to keep, and I didn't want to be the one who told you. It killed me every moment we were together and even more when we were apart because all I wanted to do was this." She pressed her lips to Gavin's in a gentle but passionate kiss, and his irritation melted.

Chapter 33

The first evening of the Clan Gathering had finally arrived, and the house was quieter than it had been in a week-other than Beatrice and the kitchen staff. They were still going strong. Beatrice excused herself from the fray and disappeared into her room to dress for the festivities.

She always loved this time of year, because she could see the enjoyment of her hard work play out on all of the faces of the people she loved. They didn't keep a staff at the estate during the year except for her and Braeden. They did employ a couple of housekeepers but they didn't live there like she and Braeden did. They just came a couple days a week to clean the main rooms and do laundry.

But during the weeks leading up to the gathering, the house was full of staff who stayed on the property because they worked such late nights. The house was so alive... so full of life and energy. It was as it should be. And this year was even more enjoyable because Rebecca was here. Beatrice couldn't help but to be thrilled that Rebecca's *sudden* visit coincided with this event. There was no way she could have planned that any better if she had tried.

She took one last look in the mirror and nodded satisfactorily at her attire. Braeden would be pleased.

She laid out Braeden's evening kilt jacket, kilt and vest on the bed and retrieved a second kilt and dress jacket that she needed to deliver to Gavin.

On her way out the door, her eyes landed on the photo of her, Gavin, Braeden, Maggie and Maggie's daughter, Fiona when the children were about ten. She missed those days. She missed Fiona and couldn't imagine losing a child- losing Gavin, who was as much her child as anyone's- and she understood the drinking. Maggie's heart had been broken, and every year the Gathering was a reminder to Maggie of that incredible loss, because it was on the way home from the Gathering, that Fiona was in the accident that took her life.

Beatrice had been so busy setting up for the event this year that she didn't have time to check on Maggie as often as she would have liked, but she had Ewan on the job so she knew that at the very least, Maggie wouldn't be alone, and she wouldn't be driving.

Beatrice hadn't had time to *encourage* Maggie to check out her suspicions regarding Gavin's birth more than just the one time she visited her at the hospital. And knowing Maggie, she had most likely forgotten all about it so Beatrice wasn't holding her breath on discovering anything new until after the Gathering.

* * *

Kara wasn't prepared for what she saw in the file room that morning. Maggie was sprawled out across a mess of papers. She shook Maggie fearing the worst but was relieved when Maggie burped a toxic mixture of bourbon and morning breath.

"What in the name o' the wee man, are you doin'?"

Without comment, Maggie stood and began shuffling through boxes of files like a lunatic. "Leave me alone with my guilt, dear. All will be revealed soon."

"Have you been drinking?"

"A bit."

Kara dropped a blanket over Maggie's shoulders. "I'll take your shift today until we can get someone else to come in."

"You're a dear. Thank ye', pet."

Kara was afraid for Maggie. She needed help. She'd never seen her like this: Agitated, keyed up, obsessed. And when she saw the file for Gavin McDermott that Maggie placed on top of one of the neater stacks, she couldn't figure out why Maggie was suddenly so obsessed over Gavin. But she didn't have time to think about any of that now since she was taking Maggie's shift for the evening.

* * *

Beatrice headed to Rebecca's room after leaving Gavin's kilt and jacket in his empty room. She joined her in front of the mirror. "You look stunning, my dear."

Rebecca trailed her fingers along the patterned fabric of her gown. "Thank you. This is a beautiful dress. Isn't it?"

"Aye. You are the Laird's daughter." The look of love on Beatrice's face nearly made Rebeca cry. "That is your tartan, you ken?"

"Yes. My…father told me."

"Well, you look bonny in McDermott colors. They suit you…My Lady." Beatrice winked playfully.

The magnanimity of Beatrice's statement sunk in. Rebecca really had a clan- a family. She was a *Lady* now. To have that as part of her title was a bit strange. Well, in fact, having *anything* that resembled a title was a bit strange. Not long ago, she was working in lumber at Boltz Hardware, and this week she was a Lady, the daughter of a Laird. Reality *really* did trump fantasy.

"You're wearing your sash in the wrong place though, Luv. May I?"

"Please."

After Beatrice finished the sash adjustments, Rebecca checked herself out in the mirror. She looked like a Scottish princess. Her hair was coiffed with perfect simplicity on top of her head and Beatrice stuck bits of heather in the jumble of curls. Rebecca couldn't help but smile.

Just then, Gavin exited the bathroom and Beatrice was struck dumb.

"Beatrice," Gavin said pointedly. Still irritated that she kept such a mammoth of a secret from him all of these years.

Beatrice looked between Gavin and Rebecca trying to discern the situation. Tears welling up in her eyes. "Aye. Please tell me ye ken."

"Aye, we know the truth of it."

Beatrice's tears spilled onto her cheeks. "I am so relieved."

There was no way that Gavin could stay angry with this woman no matter what she did, and he enveloped her into a hearty hug. "So am I. Believe me."

After Beatrice composed herself, she patted Gavin on the cheek. "Your kilt is in your room."

"Ah. Thank you, Mum."

"You are welcome, my sweet boy."

Gavin gave Rebecca a kiss on his way out the door. "I think it's time I spoke to my father."

Beatrice nodded her agreement. "You best get on with that. He's in his suite." Gavin winked at Rebecca and left.

Beatrice set the remaining heather on Rebecca's table. "And I have to drag Braeden toward the shower or he'll never be ready in time."

After she was alone, Rebecca stood in front of the mirror for a very long time and just stared at the woman looking back...At this Scotswoman. There was no denying that she was Scottish now. She had a clan. She belonged. The person looking back at her was very different, more self-confident than she was just a few weeks ago. Maybe self-confidence wasn't the exact word she was looking for. Maybe it was self-acceptance.

She did accept who she was before, but it seemed that it always hinged on whether she was satisfied in whatever relationship she was in at the moment.

* * *

"Father." Gavin bellowed as he slammed through the door to the library. The moment James saw Gavin's face he knew his son knew the truth. He stood slowly and squared his shoulders for battle. "Why?!"

James took a solid breath. "I know you don't agree with my methods but I will not apologize for withholding this information from you."

"Surely, there would have been an appropriate time to tell me the truth over the past twenty years. I can understand withholding while I was young but…" Gavin paced and then stopped abruptly, locking eyes with James. "So let me just be overly clear so there aren't any *more* misunderstandings about what we are actually talking about. I'm not your actual, bio-logical, blood son."

"No, but make no mistake, you are my son."

"Not biologically though."

"Correct, not biologically."

Gavin steeled his eyes at James. "You're certain?"

"Yes."

"Who is my father?"

James sat down. "I don't know."

"Then how did you discover the truth?"

James gestured to the other chair. "Sit." Noticing Gavin's resistance, he urged him again. "Please."

James took another settling breath as Gavin sat uncom-fortably across from him. "How long have you known this?"

"Remember the car accident when you were a toddler?"

"When mum died."

"Yes. You were very poorly. You had damaged your spleen. They needed my blood, you see." James took a breath and soldiered on. "And we weren't a match."

Gavin stood again because there was no way he could stay seated. "So my mum…"

James nodded slowly. "It is a possibility. Although, Beatrice and Braeden vehemently disagree with me on that subject."

"So you truly have no idea?"

"Truly." James stood and faced Gavin. "I loved you then, and I love you now. You were already the son of my heart so I made you my son on paper. I *chose* you to be my heir." James gave his words a moment to sink in before he proceeded. "But I didn't want to tell you the truth until you were a peer in your own right. I wanted you to have that…for you. That is a title you have earned by being a good and upstanding man. If someone were to contest your validity to this estate, I didn't want you left with nothing to show for it."

James continued to watch the emotions roll from Gavin's face as Gavin processed the information.

Gavin's posture softened just slightly which gave James a bit of comfort as Gavin stared at him in painful silence. James was afraid to move or breathe for fear that his heart and life would shatter before his eyes.

Gavin took the first breath and spoke quietly. "You knew I'd never go through with the peerage if I knew the truth."

James could only nod.

"I would not have been left with nothing. I was taught how to be a real man from the greatest man I know. You have given me more than a title. You have given me love and knowledge and for that I will always be grateful. I never sought a title. I never cared for one as you know." Gavin gave *his* words time to sink in before he continued. "But title or no…estate or no…You are the only father I have known, and for that, I am eternally grateful."

And then, James hugged him. They were both as equally shocked by the overt display of affection.

Gavin laughed. "You've been spending time with the American, Aye?"

James pulled back and smiled sheepishly. "Aye. She's a gift, that one." James' look spoke volumes of understanding.

"Aye. She certainly is that."

Chapter 34

Rebecca stood at the balcony that overlooked the foyer and watched Gavin and James greet the incoming guests.

The plan was for her to wait until most everyone had arrived. James wanted the clansmen and women to be mostly settled before she joined them all in the tent so he could make the announcement of her parentage to everyone and not have to field hundreds of questions at the door.

She snapped a few photos of everyone milling around and especially of Gavin and James in their kilts. She didn't know what any of the technical names for the bits of clothing Gavin was wearing were, but she loved the way his socks and the boots -laced all of the way up to just below his knees- hugged his calves. And his legs were amazing. Even his knees were sexy. It was truly amazing to her that Gavin, wearing what basically boiled down to a dress for men, looked more virile and powerful than he ever had before. And that was impossible. Well, maybe a close second to this afternoon when he was wearing the horse blanket. And damn…that kiss. She couldn't wait to be alone with him again.

Every time she heard his deep, rich voice her heart skipped a beat and when they made eye contact…time stopped. Thankful that she didn't have to pretend he was her sibling anymore, she looked her fill and didn't care.

Rebecca didn't see anyone enter for several minutes, so she descended the stairs.

James' eyes were as big as saucers when he saw Rebecca wearing the dress they picked out. The McDermott tartan suited her. James wiped a tear from his eye and Rebecca thought her heart would burst with emotion. She knew he loved her and accepted her and was happy that she was here.

When Rebecca looked at Gavin...well, the way he looked at her set her heart on fire. She couldn't tear her eyes away. She was, most definitely, in love with him.

Gavin nearly fainted at the sight of her. She was the most beautiful woman he had ever seen in his life and by the way she was looking at him...She was the real package. Smart, determined, honest and beautiful. And when she smiled, she lit up the entire room.

She curtseyed for fun and smirked at James. "Thank you for the gown. It's beautiful."

James could barely move. He was so enamored by this creature before him- his daughter. "You are welcome. And... you are beautiful."

Gavin leaned close to her ear. His breath hot on her neck. "You are stunning." She tipped her face up and he kissed her- breaking the kiss moments later at the uncomfortable throat clearing coming from James.

"I'm delighted you two have come to terms, but can you save that for *after* the announcements please?"

They smiled their consent, and James offered Rebecca his arm and led her toward the large tent where everyone was gathered. She was the luckiest, most blessed person alive.

The staff had set up a large dance floor and an area for a band at one end of the tent, and there were tables filled with food at the other end. The lights hanging throughout the tent lent an air of mystery and magic and everyone was dancing and singing and having an amazing time.

Except for Maggie.

* * *

Maggie was in a state. She had to speak with Beatrice to tell her what she discovered. She was determined to confess all of her sins to her good friend, and no one, not even dear Ewan, would stop her this time. She spotted Beatrice across the dance floor and made a beeline toward her, but was diverted by Ewan who handed her a pint and gently guided her toward the food.

"They got yer favorites here Mags. Hungry?"

"I could eat."

Ewan loaded two plates and carried them to a table in the corner. Beatrice nodded her thanks and the evening continued smoothly *for the time being.*

Chapter 35

Sean was grateful to Rebecca for the invitation. He made a quick stop at home to get dressed before he headed over. Thankfully, he thought ahead and brought a kilt and jacket with him from Glasgow. You just never knew when you would need one.

He knocked on the large front doors, and when no one answered, he pushed them slowly open. "Hello?"

The foyer was empty, so he followed the noise to a large tent in the back garden filled with people.

He looked around to see if Patrick had arrived, but he didn't see him and hadn't seen his van in the parking lot. He patted his breast pocket to assure himself that the warrant to search Patrick's van was secure. Sean wasn't even certain if Patrick would be in attendance or not, and he hoped that if he were there, he wouldn't suspect that Sean suspected him of anything regarding the bees. He just wanted to talk to him first...*feel him out* as it were.

*   *   *

The Gathering was in full swing, and the entire town seemed to be enjoying themselves immensely. Rebecca was filled with a mix of emotions as she overlooked the people of the town- her town.

The event began with a mournful tune on the bagpipes, which to Rebecca's happy surprise was played by her former neighbor, Archie. He played as he walked in and through the tables in his kilt, knobby knees proudly displayed, and other than Rebecca, who had no idea what was going on, everyone's heads were bowed and eyes were closed during this reverent moment.

After this, James stood, and the group stayed quiet. He gave a speech of prosperity for the next year and ended with, "I have two wonderful announcements to make if you will all permit me a few minutes."

After many nods and murmurs of approval, James began. "Many of you know that Gavin, my son, was to receive a peerage. It was just announced at the House of Lords yesterday. Gavin now holds the title of Lord McDermott in his own right."

The clan erupted in applause, and Gavin forced a smile. "Thank you. You are all too kind."

Rebecca was close enough to see his jaw clench. He didn't look particularly happy to be the center of attention.

James smiled her way. "There is someone I'd like to introduce you to." He held out his hand and she took it. It was so warm and comforting. She hadn't noticed how thick his fingers were until she had her hand in his but did notice that his hand was huge and very strong, and she felt safe. He pulled Rebecca toward the front of the stage.

Everyone grew absolutely quiet and James looked around the room at his clansmen with pride. "This beautiful young lady standing before you is my daughter Rebecca. I acknowledge her publicly, and as such, she will be Lady McDermott." And the clapping began again.

She caught her breath. She realized that nothing had felt entirely real until this moment. Surreal? Definitely. Sure she knew in her head that James was her father, but the reality never entirely hit her not even when Beatrice mentioned it just hours before. But when her father called her Lady McDermott, she teared up. She rarely got emotional about anything, but this…This was different. This was raw. This was real.

The clansmen took off their hats and bowed in unison. The women curtsied, and she stood there like a statue until Gavin placed his hand on her lower back and whispered to her that she should smile and curtsey back. She held a death grip on his arm as she did so she wouldn't fall over mid dip, and thankfully, she executed a fairly decent curtsey.

James looked to Gavin for silent approval and Gavin nodded back. James waited for silence once again and took a deep breath. "There is one last order of business we need to clear up if you will give me a few minutes to muddle through this.

He downed a tot of whiskey and looked over his clansmen. "We've all established that Gavin is my son and that he, in his own right, is Lord McDermott. What has not been made clear is that Gavin is in fact…" He looked to Gavin again who gave him a reassuring nod. "Gavin has been adopted. By me. As such, he is my heir to this estate and the titles that come with it, and that cannot be contested. He is my son. He has always been my son."

"Why tell us this now?" yelled Archie from the back of the room.

All heads turned back in questioning silence to James. He looked at Gavin and Rebecca and smiled at them as the picture they presented was not one of filial love. They were clearly attracted to -and most likely, in love with- one another. He gestured in their direction. "I should think the answer to that question was quite obvious." He smiled warmly at Gavin and Rebecca.

The crowd yelled and clapped, and Gavin and Rebecca obliged them with a brief kiss.

Not awkward at all. Rebecca was amazed by the way the clan received all of their Laird's life-altering news. She figured these announcements were just a formality, a show of respect to James' friends and family who have known Gavin for his entire life, but she didn't think they'd go over as smoothly. However, they all seemed eager to get on with the festivities.

After the formality of the meal was concluded, everyone milled about and chatted or participated in the various available activities. This first day consisted of a dance and on the lawn the athletes were getting in one last practice for the main event of the festivities that would take place starting tomorrow morning. The Highland Games.

Kilts were flying up everywhere and it was true what they say about the Scots. She saw more butts than she ever cared to. A large group of men were hurling stones and throwing giant tree trunks across the grass. This was affectionately known as the caber. There were a few women hurling the stones as well, but none seemed interested in practicing for the caber toss.

A bag piper began playing, and Rebecca was transfixed by the sword dancers' skill and stamina. She'd never seen anything like it.

Every year, Archie brought a small portion of his herd of Highland cattle with him to the estate just to lend some authenticity and ambience to the festivities, and it gave the cows a chance to graze a different pasture for a week or so. It also gave Archie much to do during the festivities because, according to local rumor, the cows rarely did what they were supposed to do, which was to stay in the pasture. Before long, Archie would be seen traipsing across the green expanse with a cow or two in tow. Today was no exception. One cow was perilously close to the parking lot, and there were two others that had decided that the bagpipes were an enticement. Those horns could be extremely dangerous if they were left unattended, and Archie was doing his best to round them up and drag them away from the tent.

Later, a band took the stage and everyone started dancing. Rebecca had a difficult time finding a beat in the music with the bagpipes screeching through the drums and flute and violin, and she wasn't quite sure what the people on the dance floor were doing. She assumed they were dancing. Although, she wasn't really sure.

Their gyrations and odd twitching movements were YouTube-worthy.

James stepped up next to her. "Care to dance?"

"I have no idea how to dance like that." It wasn't false modesty speaking. She could dance, she was actually quite good.

"Nobody does."

That made her laugh. "Sure. I'm game if you are." She let him lead her to the dance floor, and she tried to follow his lead as he twisted her around the floor. She had never felt more uncoordinated in her life.

"You are getting the hang of it."

She laughed. There was no way she would ever get the hang of this. "We can agree to disagree."

James threw his head back and laughed and spun her again. She was having fun. She laughed more out of joy than embarrassment so all was good in the world.

When the dance ended she hugged him, and Gavin very gallantly tapped James on the shoulder.

"My turn."

Rebecca smiled and was relieved to hear them play a waltz, which sounded so unusual with the bagpipes.

Gavin couldn't take his eyes off of her. And he could hardly believe that she was truly available to him. He vowed in his heart to never let her go. To America or otherwise.

Patrick arrived late- as usual- and was shocked to see Gavin smiling and dancing with Rebecca. Didn't he realize that he was nothing now? That he had no father? How could he be so happy knowing that his entire life was a lie?

He caught Gavin's eye. Gavin seemed oddly unaffected which pissed him off. He'd have to do something about that. When the dance ended, Patrick sauntered up to him prepared to pour salt in the wound he knew he had opened up but was cut off by Inspector O'Brian.

"Patrick, can I have a word?"

Patrick tried not to look guilty, but it was nearly impossible because he knew what he held in the back of his van, could do some definite damage to his *clean* record. He ignored the Inspector and walked the other way. But the moment the Inspector asked about looking in the back of his van, Patrick knew he needed to get the hell out of there. So he bolted.

Gavin saw the exchange between Sean and Patrick. He didn't know what Sean said to him, but once Patrick took off, he saw an opportunity to help Sean catch him. He kissed Rebecca on the cheek and ran in the opposite direction in an effort to cut Patrick off, hopefully giving Sean time to grab him. But Patrick had always been a fast runner.

Braeden, never one to be left out of the fun, saw the commotion, and extended his leg, tripping Patrick up. Patrick face-planted near the dance floor where the exhibitors had stored their decorative swords.

If one were to ask Patrick why he thought picking up a sword at that moment was a good idea, he would not have had a sufficient answer for them as he wasn't thinking things through just then. He sliced his sword through the air.

Smirking at each other like adolescent boys, Gavin and Sean both lunged for swords of their own and shouted "En Garde" in unison causing a large group of drunk, spectating clansmen to cheer and laugh loudly, clearly excited for the *obviously planned* theatrical display.

Patrick wasn't amused. "I'm not goin' to jail."

Sean shrugged. "I never said you were but now it really looks as if you might be. Do you think you could put the sword down and chat a bit?"

"And have you arrest me? No thanks." He lunged at Gavin but thankfully, Gavin deflected the thrust and stepped back.

And then it was on. The swishing and pinging of metal on metal rang throughout the tent, calling spectators to the "show." Rebecca and Kara- who had arrived moments before- caught up to the action just as the fight was exiting the large tent and spilling out onto the sprawling lawn. Jab, guard, turn, parry, spin...

"How much sexier can he be?" Rebecca said mostly to herself as she watched Gavin's back muscles strain against his jacket.

"I don't think it's possible." Kara answered. And Rebecca realized Kara wasn't looking at Gavin. She was locked on Sean. A small smile of understanding creased Rebecca's face.

Spin, thrust, parry, guard...Patrick was losing this battle, and he knew it, so when the opportunity arose, he dropped his sword and hightailed it to his parked van.

Gavin and Sean split up trying to impede his progress but Rebecca, being able to see the big picture from her vantage point, knew that if they couldn't prevent Patrick from reaching his car, he would be in the wind.

Rebecca hiked up her skirts and ran toward her car. She didn't really think ahead as to what she planned to do when she got in her car but she figured she could at least try to block the exit over the bridge before Patrick could reach freedom.

Before she reached her car, she saw Sean and Gavin barreling on foot toward the bridge to block Patrick's van from crossing, followed by Biscuit who, by the sound of his barking and howling, thought this was great fun. To add to the chaos, Archie was frantically trying to remove his cow from the parking lot but the stubborn creature would have none of it. And he was directly in Patrick's path as well.

"What the hell are they thinking?" Rebecca yelled to no one in particular. It looked like they were going to try to stop his exit with their bodies, which would most definitely end up very poorly for both Gavin and Sean. They didn't look like they had the mind to step out of the way, so Rebecca did the only thing she could think of, and that was to ram headlong into Patrick's van with her car. Rebecca slammed her car into first gear and flew toward Patrick's van, praying she could get there before Patrick did bodily damage to the men...or the cow.

The sound of crunching metal was deafening, and the pain of slamming into the airbag was something Rebecca hadn't thought of before she took matters into her own hands. That thing hurt, but the alternative *smashing into the steering wheel* would be decidedly worse. She assessed her *functionality* and nearly cried in thanks that she was relatively unscathed.

"Rebecca!" Gavin yelled as he rushed toward her to remove her from the crushed car. "My God! Are you alright?"

Rebecca nodded and exited the car to a warm, kilted, warrior man hug which she snuggled into willingly...That was, until the comforting arms were replaced by two hands at her shoulders, gripping and shaking her for dear life. "What the hell were you thinking?!"

"I could ask you the same thing." Rebecca scolded as she removed herself from Gavin's death-grip. "Standing in front of his van? Did you actually think he would stop? He..."

Their disagreement was abruptly interrupted by a familiar buzzing sound. Rebecca didn't wait to pinpoint where the noise was coming from. She ran the other way. But this time, it wasn't her voice screaming in pain, it was Patrick's.

The jostling of the van dislodged several of the beehives that Patrick, apparently, still had contained in the back of his van, and now his cab was filling with bees. Patrick basically flew out of the van and ran around flailing his arms, trying to get the bees away from him.

"Stop! Watch where you're headed, lad!" Archie continued to yank on the cow to get it to move, but it had other plans.

Evelynn wailed, "Oh no Archie, My love!" in the distance. But to no avail…Patrick wasn't watching where he was going and broadsided the Highland cow, knocking himself to the ground, making it very easy for Sean to finally handcuff him.

* * *

Officer Reid drove his police car over the bridge just in time to see Patrick slam into the side of the cow. He roared in laughter.

Reid retrieved Patrick from Sean and deposited him in the back of the police car. Since Patrick wasn't focusing on escaping any longer, and since there were clearly bees in the back of Patrick's van, Sean knew they would have a good amount of evidence to convict Patrick for the many thefts over the past few years.

Rebecca made it back to the safety of the gathered crowd and sought out her family. Beatrice patted her cheek. "Oh luv. Are you alright?"

"Yes. I'm fine." She smiled at the scene wrapping up and watched the police car take Patrick down the road. Gavin and Sean began heading back.

James wrapped an arm around her shoulder. "You've proved yourself a true Celt today. Jumping into the fray."

Rebecca smiled at the compliment.

Ewan tipped back a beer laughing as he recalled Rebecca ramming her car into Patrick's van. "That was bloody excellent!"

Braeden could barely speak for the tears of amusement trailing down his cheeks. "That was the best entertainment I've had in years!"

Ewan clinked his glass to Braeden's. "Aye. Nothing like a dinner and a show."

By the time Gavin and Sean returned to the group, the six of them, including Kara and Ned, were all in stitches, laughing off the stress of the near-disaster. Kara didn't waste any time aligning herself next to Sean, and they struck up a heated conversation about the NHS and its flaws.

Chapter 36

Maggie was fit to be tied. She was drunk and she was tired of being put off. If Beatrice wouldn't listen, she'd have to go straight to the Laird himself. She saw him standing near Gavin and Sean. She grabbed a few shots of whiskey that had been left over on a table and threw them back for courage.

"Milord?"

"Maggie! Leave the man alone." Beatrice tried to pull Maggie away but she resisted.

"I cannae. I need to account for my sins." Maggie crossed herself and spat on the ground. "Lord McDermott?"

"Yes, Maggie?"

This was it. Maggie thought. It was now or never. She avoided eye contact with Beatrice because she knew she'd be staring daggers at her and she'd come too far to turn back now. "Uh…Well…How should I say this? Gavin is not your son."

James nodded. "We have just recently established that Gavin most certainly is my son."

"Gavin is not your son…Because Sean is."

James couldn't believe what he was hearing. "What? How on earth do you know that?"

Gavin wasn't sure he heard her correctly. "What are you saying?"

Sean knew he had just entered some alternate reality. He was born here sure, but the son of a Laird? "What?"

Beatrice threw her hands into the air. "I knew it!"

James put a comforting hand on Maggie's shoulder. "Perhaps you should start from the beginning, Maggie."

"Aye. I suppose I should." Maggie took a deep breath, grabbed the half pint of beer from Ewan's hand and tossed it back before he could protest. "The day Gavin was born, the rain was coming down hard- lightning and hail…so much wind." She eyeballed the small crowd of people surrounding her. "I was just about to band your wee bairn when the lights went out. I couldnae see a thing. I went into the hall and an orderly practically threw another wee lad at me. I set the babes down together in a warming bassinet to tag them. And I uh…may have mixed up the two sets of identification bands. I remember the date perfectly because it was my *first* sobriety date. May 20th."

Kara looked at her sideways.

Maggie shrugged. "Had a wee bit of a relapse."

"Let me just…" James grabbed Kara's shot of whiskey and tossed it back. "So you're saying…Can someone bring me another whisky?"

Maggie handed him one off a nearby table. "So kind, Maggie. Thank you." He chugged it back as well. "So you mean to say Inspector O'Brian there is actually my son?"

"Aye. He most definitely is."

James shook his head to try to make some sense out of everything. "This is a trifle sudden."

"You think?" Sean didn't see this coming. Neither did anyone else. Except maybe Beatrice. She had a very triumphant look about her. Maggie, as far as he'd witnessed in the short time he'd been in the Highlands, was always drunk so he was still skeptical whether his DNA would confirm that he was James's son. He did look a lot like the Laird though. And now that he was thinking about it, he looked a lot like Rebecca as well.

James turned to Sean. "Let me have a look at you."

Sean's mind was blown, but he stood there and looked back at James. Of course, Sean would insist on a paternity test, but when Rebecca threw her arms around him and hugged him like he was a long lost friend, he prayed that the test would reveal that he was truly part of the family.

Beatrice was so pleased with how everything turned out. She couldn't have planned this better if she tried.

Chapter 37

Once the shock of Sean's paternity wore off, the topic of conversation gradually turned to other things and Gavin found the opportunity to whisk Rebecca away for the sunset. Because who doesn't love a romantic sunset? The weather was beautiful, so Gavin suggested they take a ride on the ATV up to "their spot to have a wee chat."

Rebecca kissed him in agreement, hiked up her skirts and sat behind Gavin, wrapping her arms familiarly around his waist. "I'd like that a lot."

Gavin desperately wanted to make sure that Rebecca was open to staying in Scotland indefinitely. He had to admit, he was a tad bit nervous broaching the subject of her leaving everything she was familiar with in the U.S. in order to stay with him, but he was hopeful that she considered Scotland, and the estate, her home and wouldn't want to leave. He didn't think his heart could take it if she left for good.

They parked and walked to the top of the cliff hand in hand. Rebecca gasped as she took in the beauty before them. The air was crisp but not uncomfortable. The sun had set, but the moon was brighter and larger than either one of them ever thought was possible. It was as though it was placed in front of them for this single moment, and to Gavin, this was the most powerful, most beautiful moment he had ever seen, primarily because he was standing next to Rebecca.

They stood silent for a long while until Gavin broke it with a purposeful throat-clearing. "You know, we could really use your help around the place, and you're so good with grout."

"Yes, I am..."

"And I have never seen anyone wield a hammer quite like you."

"I am gifted." She smiled warmly and caressed his unshaven cheek. "You sure know how to sweet-talk the ladies."

"Aye. It's a gift." Gavin wrapped his arms around her and pulled her close. He kissed her on the forehead, afraid to say what was really causing him heartache. The thought of losing her.

"The house needs you- desperately."

"It will never be finished."

"That's what I'm counting on."

That really was one of the sweetest things Rebecca had ever heard.

Gavin nuzzled her neck. "Plus. there's the thing with Biscuit. He has grown very accustomed to you, as well."

"I wouldn't want to disappoint him."

"No. He would be heartbroken if you left."

"I can only imagine." She looked up, trying to catch a full view of him without leaving the warmth of his arms. "So out with it. What are you trying to say, Gavin?"

Gavin stepped back to arms-length so he could see her beautiful face in the moonlight. "I'm trying to ask you if you are going back to America, or if you are planning on staying in Scotland, with me...uh...us. Your family."

He was truly magnificent. His vulnerability broke her heart, but thankfully, she had decided to stay in Scotland indefinitely. She had fallen in love with Gavin, she had finally found the perfect, very much in need, fixer-upper project that would keep her busy for decades, and she could still pursue her writing career if she stayed in Scotland. She'd be an idiot if she chose otherwise. The most important reason...being in love with Gavin.

"I have to head to the U.S…" His face dropped and she felt terrible for starting her sentence that way. "But it's only to pack up my stuff so I can move it here…indefinitely."

Gavin was too overcome to speak so he gathered her in his arms and kissed her with his entire being. To say that their kiss was passionate would be an understatement.

They were both breathless when he pulled back. "You know this means you are stuck with all of us forever?"

She couldn't take her eyes off of him. "I am more than OK with that." She pulled him into another heart-stopping kiss.

After the sun had set, they rejoined the mass of kilted humanity on the back garden. Beatrice was beaming when she saw them walking hand-in hand. "Lad, I cannot tell ye how happy I am." She grinned at Rebecca and patted her cheek. "You'll forgive an old lady for embellishing a wee bit on the Laird's *heart attack* won't ya?"

"No, I won't."

Beatrice's countenance fell and Rebecca laughed. "There's nothing to forgive you for. I have you to thank for bringing me here in the first place." She whispered in her ear. "Just wondering. Did you have anything to do with the flood in my cottage?"

Beatrice's eyes grew wide and she checked her watch. "Oh would ya look at the time I…"

Rebecca launched herself at Beatrice and wrapped her in a hug then whispered a thank you. "I couldn't imagine living anywhere else."

Rebecca and Gavin joined the others at the table and Rebecca looked around at the wonderful gift of family that had been given to her. The joy in the air was tangible and Rebecca was content to bask in it while listening to James confirm Sean's paternity. "Although I'm certain that you are my son, I do agree with you that it is better to get the DNA test earlier rather than later."

Sean nodded. "I will set up the test."

"And when it is confirmed, I will make the announcement the next time the clan gathers over Christmas." James nodded toward Gavin and Rebecca. "It seems I may have another announcement to make at that time as well."

Rebecca looked at Gavin and smiled then she nodded at James. His heart nearly burst with joy that she would agree to marry him- when he asked her. Which he decided should be post-haste since his dad just basically did it for him and Beatrice would not be far behind. He kissed her soundly for good measure and whispered…"I will ask you myself at some point."

His warm breath sent chills down Rebecca's spine, and she stroked his cheek. "And I will tell you 'yes, with all of my heart' when that time comes."

Beatrice watched with joy as Gavin reverently kissed Rebecca and knew that the love they held for each other was the stuff of legends.

Epilogue

James stood at the head of the massive table covered with Christmas decorations and waited for the group to quiet down. "May I have your attention please?"

Eventually, they quieted down and James was able to continue. "I just want it to be made known that certain *additional* truths have come to light regarding another member of this family."

The murmurers wondered if Rebecca was pregnant.

"I have another son to introduce you to. The man you see standing next to me, you all know as inspector Sean O'Brien from Glasgow. We have confirmed his paternity with certainty, but you'd all agree that the resemblance between the good Inspector and my Rebecca is quite remarkable, regardless of the test results." There were nods of agreement. "We found out this truth because of some excellent sleuthing. Maggie, thank you for exposing this truth. You have blessed this old man more than you know."

Maggie blushed and received the bursts of praise and congratulations from the group. She was thankful and exceedingly relieved that he didn't reveal her part in the mix up.

He continued. "Not that you need my permission to gossip about anything and everything, but I give you my blessing to spread the word. Please welcome Sean, my new son, to the family."

Everyone clapped and shouted their congratulations. The ruckus went on for nearly a minute, and Sean was beaming from ear-to-ear. The entire family was beaming. In truth,

Sean had become an integral part of the community even before this announcement. He and Gavin had become fast, friends initially bonding over their failure to get a MacNab during the gathering, but Sean had also been very interested in learning about tending the bees, which both Gavin and Braeden were only too eager to teach him.

Rebecca and Sean fell seamlessly into their siblinghood, and both learned that they were master-pranksters. Something James had been known for in his youth. Which, according to Beatrice, "May or may not have had anything to do with the reason he was *asked to leave* Eton."

Sean transferred to the Highlands on a permanent basis, which, to Chief Inspector Hollister, was the best sort of idea.

Also, the fact that Sean was now dating Kara didn't hurt anything in terms of integrating himself into the community. *But that's another story.*

James wasn't entirely finished with the announcements. "I am a most fortunate man. I have three beautiful children and…" James glanced at Rebecca and Gavin with a smirk. "It seems that I may have forgotten something of great import. Gavin, perhaps you could help jog my memory?"

Gavin pulled Rebecca to him and kissed her left hand, which sported a very large engagement ring.

"Ah yes. Gavin and Rebecca are engaged and will be married in April." The room erupted in cheers and well-wishes.

Rebecca was in heaven, and she fully believed that reality trumped fantasy…every time.

Two years later. A final note from Rebecca herself…

I hate it when books end just after the kiss. I hate it when movies end on the kiss. I want to know what happened to my favorite characters after the book ends.

So this is what happened…

Patrick was given 10 years in jail for crimes ranging from theft to money laundering. It was actually a miracle that he only got 10 years. He owes Gavin big time… but let's be honest, it's Patrick, He'll probably be out in 3 years.

Kara and Sean…. Again, that is another story.

Beatrice and Braeden are still running the estate. Braeden can now simply focus on the job of a gillie and enjoys tending the bees in particular. Beatrice is happy in the kitchen. She loves the thought of more and more children causing havoc around the estate, and she is doing her level best to see that Sean and Kara end up together. I don't think she has resorted to property damage yet, but none of us would put it past her, and I have on more than one occasion, encouraged Kara to install a security system.

Gavin and I are very happy. We married two years ago in April, and we have an adorable baby boy (Timothy Gavin James McDermott) and another one on the way. We are very content to live and work at the estate. In the end, I didn't get the picket fence, but rock-walls are so much more durable, and I couldn't have created a better man in any of my novels, than the man I get to wake up to every morning. He is so much more than I could have ever dreamed.

My mother has been a very attentive Grandmother and is considering relocating to Scotland. I'm not sure how I feel about that.

Lacy is happily married, and they spend as many of their vacations with us in Scotland as possible.

The truffles are just a couple years away from becoming a profitable business, and we just signed a contract with Harrods' to distribute our honey. The proceeds from the sale of the honey have gone into rebuilding the estate -which is now flourishing, so in the end, there was no need to involve the National Trust. James was thrilled.

We recently filmed a movie at the estate and James wasn't entirely prickly to the crew. He was even asked to be an extra. He got to sit in his chair in the library and quietly read a book while the action happened in an adjoining room. He wouldn't admit to it but we all knew he was secretly very happy that he was given the opportunity to have his fifteen-minutes of fame. And he finally got his MacNab!

I completed the book about Ciro and Abigail shortly after Christmas, and it became a best-seller. I also co-authored *with Gavin of course,* a Home Repair for Dummies *in Scotland* book, and it sold very well. It is incredible how many people purchase the *For Dummies* books. Our next book will be Beekeeping for Dummies. I'm working on a more contemporary romantic novel, but my life is so amazing now, there's no way I could ever write anything close.

Oh…and we all lived happily ever after.

Acknowledgments

Writing may appear to be a solitary undertaking, but it is not- at least for me anyway. I am grateful to everyone who has helped me along this path.

I have had such incredible good fortune to be surrounded by the most fantastic people. My husband, Paul and my children, Jordan, Rachel and Joshua…Thank you for always being available to toss story ideas around with me! You are all brilliant. Thank you Kristi Odman and Shannon Lamarche; you were on this from the beginning and I am so grateful for your encouragement and fab line editing. Thank you Sandra Perez Gluschankoff, bringer of conflict and amazing editor. You are a genius and I could not have done this without you. Thank you Finola Hughes for your brilliant input, astute guidance and copious amounts of tea…and Ian Buchannan, thank you for "Scottishizing" the dialogue. Thank you Doug Johnson for taking this book under your Cave Moon Press wing. Thank you Mom and Rose for teaching me how to spell and to read. It came in handy more than once during this endeavor. You are loved.

There are so many others who have given me their support on this endeavor from early on, and I would be remiss if I did not mention them because they are all truly irreplaceable: Sandy Sfeir, Dori Zuckerman, Carlyne Grager, Cindy Stevens, Michelle Magers, Ross McCall, Jonathan Rhys Meyers and Tracy Spiridakos. THANK YOU!

And…Now that I have finally finished, you can all stop *encouraging* me to *get on with it.*